John M[ilton]

SAMSON AGONISTES

EDITED BY

SIR EDMUND K. CHAMBERS

K.B.E., C.B., D.Litt.

Sometime Scholar of Corpus Christi College, Oxford

[BL]ACKIE & SON LIMITED

LONDON AND GLASGOW

BLACKIE & SON LIMITED
  16/18 William IV Street.
    Charing Cross, London, W.C.2
  17 Stanhope Street, Glasgow

BLACKIE & SON (INDIA) LIMITED
  103/5 Fort Street, Bombay

BLACKIE & SON (CANADA) LIMITED
  Toronto

Printed in Great Britain by Blackie & Son, Ltd., Gla.

PREFACE

The merits of *Samson Agonistes* as a school-book, especially for those who desire to obtain a knowledge of the spirit of the Greek drama without learning Greek, stand in need of no justification. The present editor has attempted to give, in Introduction and Notes, just so much information and comment as may help and not hamper the student. The accumulation of classical parallels he has regarded as of little educational value. Some remarks upon metre and grammar have been added in Appendices, where no one need read them who does not wish. Gratitude is due to previous editors, notably to Todd, to Professor Masson, to Mr. Churton Collins, and to Mr. A. W. Verity; also to the late Dr. Bradshaw for his *Concordance to Milton*, and to Mr. Robert Bridges for his helpful tractate on *Milton's Prosody*

Blackie's Standard English Classics

With Introduction and Notes

A Selection

BYRON—**Childe Harold's Pilgrimage. Cantos I and II.** T. S. Sterling, M.A., and J. W. Holme, M.A.

BROWNING—**Strafford.** Agnes Wilson.

CHAUCER—**The Nonne Prest his Tale.** R. F. Patterson, M.A., D.Litt.
The Pardoner's Tale. W. C. Robb.
The Prologue to the Canterbury Tales. R. F. Patterson, M.A., D.Litt.

Contemporary Short Stories. Edited by E. R. Wood, B.A.

DICKENS—**Short Stories from Dickens.** J. G. Fyfe, M.A.

English Essays. A Representative Anthology. W. Cuthbert Robb, M.A.

GOLDSMITH—**The Citizen of the World.** Selected Letters. W. A. Brockington, M.A.
She Stoops to Conquer. H. Littledale, M.A., Litt.D.

KINGLAKE—**Eothen.** Including the Author's own notes.

MACAULAY—**Essay on Milton.** John Downie, M.A.

MARLOWE—**Dr. Faustus.** R. G. Lunt, M.A.(Oxon.).
Edward the Second. R. G. Lunt, M.A.(Oxon.).

MILTON—**Lycidas.** H. B. Cotterill.
Paradise Lost. Books I, II, III, VI. (In separate vols.).
Paradise Lost. Books I and II. F. Gorse, M.A. (In one vol.).
Samson Agonistes. Sir Edmund K. Chambers, K.B.E., C.B., M.A., D.Litt.

Modern Short Essays. Compiled by James M. Charlton, M.A.

POPE—**Rape of the Lock.** Frederick Ryland, M.A.

Prelude to Modern Prose. M. W. Pitt, M.A.(Oxon.).

SCOTT—**The Lady of the Lake. The Lay of the Last Minstrel.**

SHERIDAN—**The Critic.** R. F. Patterson, M.A., D.Litt.

SPENSER—**The Faery Queene.** Book II. W. Keith Leask, M.A.
The Faery Queene. Book V. E. H. Blakeney, M.A.

BLACKIE & SON LIMITED, LONDON AND GLASGOW

Printed in Great Britain by Blackie & Son, Ltd., Glasgow

CONTENTS

CONTENTS

INTRODUCTION

I.—THE LIFE OF MILTON

John Milton was born on the 9th of December, 1608, at the sign of the Spread Eagle in Bread Street, Cheapside. Here his father followed the occupation of a scrivener. The elder Milton, also named John, came of a line of Catholic yeomen settled at Stanton St. John, in Oxfordshire. He was educated, apparently as a chorister, at Christ Church, Oxford, and became a Protestant. This led to a family quarrel. Milton went to London, adopted an honest business, and married Sarah Jeffrey, the daughter of a merchant tailor. The duty of engrossing deeds did not, however, prevent him from achieving a considerable reputation as a musician, and several specimens of his skill in the composition of madrigals and motets are preserved.

Birth and Parentage of Milton.

Young Milton, therefore, grew up in easy circumstances and a liberal atmosphere. To his father he probably owed that delight in music which he kept until his death. From the first careful attention was paid to his education. His early tutor was Thomas Young, afterwards Master of Jesus College, Cambridge; and from Young's hands he passed into St. Paul's School, then presided over by a distinguished scholar, Alexander Gill. Even as a boy, Milton applied himself to study with a vigour which injured his health. His intimate school friend was Charles Diodati, the son of an Italian physician. On April the 9th, 1625, he matriculated at Cambridge as a member of Christ's College. Here he remained until he took his M.A. degree on July the 3rd, 1632. Milton's career at Cambridge was not altogether

Milton's Education.

a success. Gossip has it that he quarrelled with his tutor,
one William Chappell, and that Chappell 'whipped' him.
It is likely enough that neither the discipline nor the pedantry
of a university were exactly congenial to Milton's independent temper. Yet there is evidence that he attained to some
distinction in the college exercises, and that, whether for his
refinement of character, or for his personal beauty, he was
nicknamed 'the lady of Christ's'.

It was originally intended that Milton should take orders;
but, at about the time he left Cambridge, he seems to have
Milton's Life at abandoned this intention, and to have already
Horton.   formed the purpose of devoting his lifetime to
the achievement of some notable work in poetry. In 1632,
at the age of twenty-three, he joined his father, who had
by now retired from business and settled down in the quiet
village of Horton, in Buckinghamshire. Here Milton dwelt
for six years, surrendering himself to the sweet influences of
the beech-woods, playing on his viol, turning over history-
books and the Greek and Latin classics, and meditating on
the poem of the future. Already, while at Cambridge, he had
composed, besides some minor and occasional verses, the *Ode
on the Nativity* in 1629. He now, in 1632, wrote *L'Allegro*
and *Il Penseroso*, two poems of country life as the scholar
felt it; and in 1633 or 1634 joined his words to the music
of Henry Lawes in the masque of *Arcades*, performed at
Harefield before the great Countess of Derby, who had once
been the subject of her kinsman Spenser's song. Another
and more ambitious effort, in which once more Milton co-
operated with Lawes, was the masque of *Comus*, performed
before Lady Derby's stepson the Earl of Bridgewater, at
Ludlow Castle, in Wales, in the September of 1634. The
tale of Milton's earlier verse is completed by *Lycidas*, an
elegy in the pastoral convention upon a college acquaintance,
Edward King, who was drowned while crossing the Irish
Channel in 1637.

In the next year Milton's rural retirement was broken by a
visit to the Continent. He set out in April, 1638, with letters
of introduction from Sir Henry Wotton, then Provost of Eton,

and others, and made his way to Paris, Florence, Rome, Naples, and Geneva. Much, both in France and Italy, must have jarred upon the austere morality of the scholar Puritan, but Milton exchanged com- *Milton in France and Italy.* pliments with the literary academies of Florence, and had notable interviews with Grotius, the famous jurist, and with Galileo. Moreover, he fell in love with a lady who is conjec- turally identified with the singer Leonora Baroni. Up to this time Milton had occupied himself chiefly with the cultivation of his intellect and the pursuit of the Muses: yet he had formed strong views on the great and agitating questions of civil and religious liberty. It was indeed, he tells us, the foresight of the coming struggle that brought him home to England, after a shorter tour than he had originally intended, in July, 1639. He did not, however, take any immediate part in political life; but neither did he return to the sylvan retire- ment of Horton. Settling down with his books in London, he undertook the tuition of his two nephews, *Milton in Lon-* Edward and John Phillips, in a 'pretty garden- *don.* house' in Aldersgate Street. Other pupils were presently added to these, and Milton's views on the theory and practice of teaching found expression in his *Letter to Mr. Samuel Hart- lib*, published in 1644. During Milton's absence in Italy his friend, Charles Diodati, had died; and on his return he com- memorated the event in his chief Latin poem, the *Epitaphium Damonis*. Nor were his intentions of serious literary achieve- ment allowed to slumber. We find him, in some note-books of this date which have been preserved, revolving innumer- able schemes for a great poem. Already *Paradise Lost* is among the subjects thought of; it is drafted in the form of a drama. But a period of over twenty years was destined to intervene between the conception and the fruition of the design; a period during which Milton was to write practically no poetry. The opening of the Long Parliament of 1640 ushered in for him a career of strenuous and *Milton a Pam-* acrimonious controversy. He espoused the cause *phleteer.* of the Presbyterian divines who wrote as Smectymnuus, and in the course of the next two years issued a series of five pamphlets, in which he inveighed against Episcopacy and the champion of Episcopacy, Bishop Hall. The most important of these was *The Reason of Church Government urged against Prelacy* (February, 1642). At the end of 1642 the Civil War broke out. The pen gave way for a time to the sword, and Milton was no soldier. Then occurred a strange and rather painful episode in his life, namely, his first marriage. In May, 1643, he took a journey into the country, and returned with a bride. She was Mary Powell, the daughter of a roistering and bankrupt Cavalier, Richard Powell, of Forest Hill, in Oxfordshire. Whatever the motive of this ill-assorted union, it turned out ill. Within a couple of months Mary Milton had quitted her home, and her husband was writing pamphlets in favour of a laxer system of divorce. These were published without a license and brought Milton into collision with the Company of Stationers. In November, 1644, appeared his finest prose work, the *Areopagitica*, an impassioned and eloquent plea in favour of a free press. Four months later he summed up his views on the divorce question in the *Tetrachordon*. The defeat of the royal cause, however, reduced the Powells to poverty, and Milton's wife sued for a reconciliation. After a somewhat dramatic scene in which she fell upon her knees before him, he consented to receive her back to a new house in the Barbican, and with her came her father, who died shortly afterwards. Four children were born to the Miltons, Anne in 1646, Mary in 1648, John, who only lived a short time, in 1651, and Deborah in 1652. The last of these cost her mother's life. In 1645 Milton had found time to publish a volume of his early English and Latin poems, but with the establishment of the Commonwealth after the execution of Charles I. on Jan. 30th, 1649, he returned to his pamphleteering. He upheld the right of the people to judge their king in his *Tenure of Kings and Magistrates*, and was shortly afterwards appointed Latin Secretary to the Council of State. It became his duty nominally to put into Latin diplomatic communications with foreign powers, actually to undertake when needful the literary defence of the

Marriage and Divorce.

The Latin Secretaryship.

new government. His first task was to answer the *Eikon
Basilike*, a work of pious meditation, composed by Charles
the First in prison, or at least published in his name.
This Milton did in the *Eikonoklastes* (1649); and was almost
immediately called upon to cross swords with Salmasius, a
learned professor of Leyden, who published in 1649 a Latin
Defensio Regia pro Carolo I. Milton replied, also in Latin,
with his *Pro Populo Anglicano Defensio* (1650). He was
attacked by Alexander Morus in the *Regii Sanguinis
Clamor ad Cœlum* (1652), but rejoined with the *Defensio
Secunda* (1654) and the *Pro Se Defensio* (1655). The controversy is not edifying on either side: it is vehemently
personal, and the range of vituperation extends from charges
of scandalous morals to imputations of bad Latinity. But
the labour expended by Milton upon such unworthy material
had a disastrous outcome in the complete loss Milton becomes
of his sight. He continued to hold his post, Blind.
but received help in the discharge of its duties, one of his
associates being the poet Andrew Marvell. In 1656 he
was married for the second time to Catherine Woodcock,
who died in the following year, and to whom a sonnet upon
her memory shows him to have been deeply attached.

Milton was not one of those who, in the closing years of the
Protectorate, felt the spirit of reaction. From a Presbyterian
he had become an Independent, but his hatred The Restora-
of prelacy was no whit abated. And if he saw tion.
the inevitable direction in which things were tending, he
wilfully closed his mind to it. He continued to write pamphlets advocating extreme and unpractical ideals. On the very
eve of the Restoration, in Feb., 1660, he published his *Ready
and Easy Way to Establish a Free Commonwealth*. By
May General Monk had declared for the Stuarts, and Milton
found it advisable to go into hiding. He fled to a friend's
house in Bartholomew's Close, where he lay throughout the
long debates over the vengeance to be taken upon the regicides. It must have been a surprise to him that he escaped
the fate to which others, far less guilty from a Royalist point
of view, were condemned. The dead bodies of Cromwell,

Ireton, and Bradshaw were dug up and subjected to indignities; General Harrison, Hugh Peters, the preacher, and a
dozen more were executed; to others minor punishment was
meted out; but though an order was issued for the burning
of Milton's books, and he was himself apparently at one time
in custody, yet his name was not amongst the number of
those finally scheduled to be exempted from the mercies of
the Indemnity Act. His escape seems to have been due to
the intrigues of Andrew Marvell, of Sir William Davenant,
of Lord Anglesey, possibly of Clarendon himself and of
others whose affection or respect the poet's noble character
and literary gifts had won him even on the Royalist side.
With the passing of the Indemnity Act, therefore, on August
the 29th, 1660, Milton was free to appear in public once
Milton in Retire- more. He retired with the wreck of his fortunes,
ment.   first to Holborn and then to a house in Lewin
Street, and devoted himself again, after a lapse of twenty
years, to letters. He was yet to live another fourteen years,
during which, though he took no part in politics, he received
the visits of many eminent men. We have gossiping accounts
of his later years from Aubrey, and from Richardson the
painter.

"I have heard many years since," says Richardson, "that he used
to sit in a gray, coarse, cloth coat at the door of his house, near Bunhill Fields, without Moorgate, in warm sunny weather, to enjoy the
fresh air, and so, as well as in his room, received the visits of people
of distinguished parts, as well as quality; and very lately I had the
good fortune to have another picture of him from an aged clergyman in
Dorsetshire, Dr. Wright. He found him in a small house, he thinks
but one room on a floor. In that up one pair of stairs, which was hung
with a rusty green, he found John Milton sitting in an elbow chair,
black clothes, and neat enough, pale but not cadaverous, his hands and
fingers gouty and with chalk-stones. Among other discourse he expressed himself to this purpose: that, was he free from the pain this gave
him, his blindness would be tolerable."

His mornings were mainly spent in study or in composition.
In the afternoon he would take exercise and recreate himself
by playing on the organ. In the evening his friends would

visit him. He supped, says Aubrey, on "olives, or some light thing; and after supper he smoked his pipe and drank a glass of water and went to bed". His habits were temperate; he "rarely drank between meals". After the blindness and the gout, his chief affliction was in his daughters. He trained them to read to him in several languages, without, it would seem, understanding the sense of what they read. We can hardly wonder that they rebelled, though it is more difficult to forgive them if it is true that they surreptitiously sold their father's books to a rag-and-bones man. Ultimately he was persuaded to send them out to get their living by embroidery in gold and silver. Milton had more comfort in his third wife, Elizabeth Minshull, whom he married in February, 1663, and who appears to have been a domesticated woman after his own heart, and a capital cook. They lived in Artillery Walk, Bunhill Fields, and during the plague of 1665 in a small cottage at Chalfont St. Giles, in Buckinghamshire, provided for them by the pains of Ellwood, the Quaker. Here Milton showed Ellwood the completed manuscript of *Paradise Lost*, and, according to the young man's account, received *The Publication of the Great Poems.* from him the suggestion of adding to it a *Paradise Regained*. Two years afterwards, after some difficulty in obtaining a license from one Thomas Tomkyns, chaplain to the Archbishop of Canterbury, *Paradise Lost* was published. Milton and his wife, who had suffered serious loss in the great fire of 1666, received for the book in all £18. It was followed by *Paradise Regained* and *Samson Agonistes* in 1671. Milton's gout proved fatal on November the 8th, 1674, and he was buried in the Church of St. Giles, Cripplegate.

II.—*SAMSON AGONISTES.*

The *Samson Agonistes* was published in the same volume as *Paradise Regained*. On a fly-leaf is the note, "Licensed, July 2, 1670". Two months later copyright was secured by the usual entry in the books of the Stationers' Company. It runs as follows:— *Publication of Samson Agonistes in 1671.*

20 Sept. [1670].

Mr. John Starkey.   Entred for his Copie, under the hands
of Mr. Tho. Tomkyns and Mr. Warden
Roper, a Copie or Booke intituled Paradise Regayn'd. A Poem in 4 Bookes.
The Author John Milton. To which is
added Samson Agonistes, A drammadic
Poem, by the same Author.

The book did not actually appear until 1671. It is an
octavo, and although both type and paper are good, is carelessly printed and punctuated. Nine lines omitted at line
1527 are supplied in a list of *Omissa*. *Samson Agonistes* has
separately numbered pages, and its own title-page. This
runs:—

SAMSON | AGONISTES | A | Dramatic Poem | THE
AUTHOR | JOHN MILTON | Aristot. Poet. Cap. 6. |
Τραγῳδία μίμησις πραξέως σπουδαίας &c. | Tragoedia est imi-
tatio actionis seriae &c.   Per misericordiam | et metum per-
ficiens talium affectuum lustrationem. | LONDON | Printed
by J. M. for JOHN STARKEY at the Mitre in | Fleet-street,
near Temple-Bar | MDCLXXI.

It has been inferred from the initials J. M. that Milton
was himself at the costs of the printing. But this is merely
a misunderstanding. The formula 'Printed by J. M. for
John Starkey' was that which had been used for a century
when the publisher of a book, instead of printing it in his
own shop, gave it out to another firm to do for him. The
printer of *Samson Agonistes* may have been John Martin.
Two other editions appeared during the 17th century—one
in 1680, and the other in 1688. They present no substantial
variations of text, except that in both the nine lines omitted
in 1571 are in their proper place.

We may distinguish in Milton's literary career three well-
marked phases. There is the period of early verse up to
Milton's return from Italy in 1639. To this belong the *Ode
on the Nativity*, *L'Allegro*, *Il Penseroso*, *Arcades*, *Comus*,

Lycidas, the *Epitaphium Damonis*. In all these Milton is the scholar and humanist, occupied mainly with literary themes, although in *Lycidas* we may note the signs of growing political and ecclesiastical interests. And throughout this period he is consciously preparing himself for the great poem that is to be. Secondly, there is the period from the opening of the Long Parliament in 1640 to the Restoration in 1660, the twenty years in which Milton was wholly and restlessly engaged in fighting the good fight, and in which all that he wrote, with the exception of a dozen sonnets, magnificent but unadorned, was rigidly and pertinaciously polemical. Thirdly, there was the period of retirement from political life which the Restoration ushered in. In the fourteen years between 1660 and his death in 1674, amid the ruin of his life-work and of his dearest hopes, old, blind, gouty, bereaved, and poor, he renewed the fires of his youth, and accomplished all and more than all that he had dreamt of in the glades of Horton.

Milton's three Literary Periods.

> "But he, though blind of sight,
> Despised, and thought extinguish'd quite,
> With inward eyes illuminated,
> His fiery virtue roused
> From under ashes into sudden flame,
> And as an evening dragon came."[1]

The brightest ornaments of the Restoration were, after all, the manifestoes of the very ideals which the Restoration came to crush. But neither *Paradise Lost* nor *Paradise Regained*, we may suppose, were directly inspired by the Restoration. The design of the greater poem, at least, must have been conceived long before. As early as 1640 or thereabouts Milton had shown his nephew Phillips one of Satan's speeches, then intended to form the opening of a drama.[2] How much more was actually written before 1660 we cannot tell; the scope of the whole is coextensive with humanity, and personal or political indications

Date of Paradise Lost.

---

[1] *S. A.*, 1687–1692.   [2] *P. L.*, iv. 32, sqq.

are rare. But it was not until 1660 that Milton had much
leisure; the opening of book iii is subsequent to the blindness which came upon him in 1652; and in that of book vii
the reference to the overthrow of the great cause is clear:

> "Standing on Earth, not rapt above the pole,
> More safe I sing with mortal voice, unchanged
> To hoarse or mute, though fallen on evil days,
> On evil days though fallen, and evil tongues,
> In darkness, and with dangers compass'd round,
> And solitude".

Paradise Regained, whether suggested by Ellwood in 1665,
as he himself thought, or not, is in any case the natural
Relation of   complement of *Paradise Lost*—the other half of
Samson Agon-   the great epic of redemption. It is therefore to
istes to the
Restoration.   *Samson Agonistes* that we must turn to find the
more intimate personal note of Milton's later life. For we
cannot doubt that he felt the Restoration deeply and intensely,
as a calamitous revolution, a complete disaster. It was the
wreck of all that he had set his faith and his hopes upon, of
all that he had worked for. The tawdry splendour of Charles's
wanton court would hardly make up to him for the loss of
liberty in Church and State. He saw his comrades executed
or imprisoned, and the bodies of those he had revered exposed to dishonour; he saw the licentiousness which the saints
had put their heels upon burst forth in unabashed triumph;
he saw the bishops whom he hated sail back to their old
pulpits in their old prelatical robes. How should his eyes
not fill with tears and his heart swell with indignation? How
should he not think that the vials of the Almighty wrath
were preparing for so faithless a generation? Of such a mood
Samson Agonistes is the record; nay, more, the expression so
outspoken that one hardly understands how the Restoration
censorship can have let it pass. In the old days, when he
was turning over and making notes of all sorts of conceivable
subjects for epic or drama, this of Samson had not failed to
suggest itself to Milton. In a note-book of about 1641 still
preserved, he has jotted down the following topics:—

"Samson pursophorus or Hybristes[1], or Samson marriing or in Ramath Lechi. Jud. 15.
"Dagonalia. Jud. 16.'

For a time he left the theme alone, but when he returned to it after 1660, it may well have seemed appropriate to his own state. For who is Samson but Milton himself, once the invincible champion, single-handed, of the Commonwealth against the hosts of her foes, now blind, bowed down in "poverty, sickness, and disease", for a while "in captivity among inhuman foes", and still "the scorn and gaze" of his enemies. Who is the Philistian Dalila, but that first wife from the royalist household, the specious beauty, the wife who was no wife while it suited her, and then came fawning to be forgiven? Who are the Philistines themselves, but the prelatical idol-worshippers who came back from over seas, with their banqueting and their drunkenness, with their "unjust tribunals" that condemned the regicides, with the "jugglers and dancers, antics, mummers, mimics" of their reopened theatres? One must beware of pressing the analogy too closely; but the intimately personal character of the main situation is patent. And, besides the denunciation, there is prophecy in the play. I do not suppose Milton to have expected that he himself should, like Samson, be in some marvellous way the minister of the divine vengeance, but that he looked for the vengeance to come, and to come quickly, that he foretold it openly and fearlessly in the midst of a hostile and unheeding generation, of that we may be certain.

Personal Note in Samson Agonistes.

> "So fond are mortal men,
> Fallen into wrath divine,
> As their own ruin on themselves to invite,
> Insensate left, or to sense reprobate,
> And with blindness internal struck."

The Stuarts were often enough "drunk with idolatry, drunk with wine", and even as Milton wrote the "spirit of frenzy"

[1] 'Samson πυρσοφόρος', or 'the Torch-bearer', clearly refers to the episode in *Judges*, xv. 4, where Samson tied firebrands to the tails of foxes, and sent them into the corn of the Philistines. 'Samson ὑβρίστης', 'the Insolent', may be an alternative title for a drama on the same subject.

was not far away. The day of reckoning for 1660 came in 1688.

Even the form of *Samson Agonistes* is in itself a protest against Restoration tendencies. Milton's attitude towards Milton and the drama is somewhat complicated, and de-the Drama. serves careful consideration. The ordinary Puritan view is simple enough. Since the middle of the sixteenth century, preachers and pamphleteers had been unsparing in their denunciations of the stage as a haunt of sin and a net of Satan. These found their extreme expression in Prynne's elaborate pamphlet of 1632, the *His-triomastix*, which for some reflections upon the queen Henrietta Maria contained in it cost him his ears. One of the first acts of the Long Parliament, when they became masters of London, was to shut up the theatres in September 1642. But Milton was no friend of Prynne's, who by an irony of fate had become an active agent of the Restoration, nor was it to be expected that the free-thinking scholar of Christ's should take precisely the same view where literature was concerned as the sour Calvinist theologian. We know that the *Arcades* and *Comus* of Milton's youth were masques, a form of drama which the stricter Puritans held in especial abhorrence; and we know from the note-books of 1641, or thereabouts, that it was still his purpose at that time to cast his great poem in a dramatic form. It has been pointed out that the opening speech was actually written, and was after-wards incorporated in *Paradise Lost*. At the same time, though Milton himself tells us that in his journeys from Horton to London he used to visit the theatres, it is probable that with growing Puritanism came a growing distaste for the kind of play that the public theatres of the seventeenth century presented. The literary merits of the Elizabethan, Jacobæan, and Caroline playwrights are high, but decency and sobriety of moral tone are not among their character-istics; they do not, in any obvious sense, make for righteous-ness. And they were all against the Puritans and for the Court. Nor were the new dramatic developments of the Restoration likely to affect Milton's condemnation. The theatres remained closed for fourteen years, from 1642 to 1656. Then performances gradually began again and were at least winked at by those in authority. In August, 1660, Charles II. granted patents to Sir William Davenant and Thomas Killigrew, who established companies respectively known as the Duke of York's and the King's. For the first time women actors appeared regularly in parts that would previously have been taken by boys; and it need hardly be said that Restoration actresses were little better than courtesans. In the plays themselves there was little to attract Milton's austere, and by this time probably somewhat conservative, taste. The tawdry tragedy of Dryden, the obscene and realistic comedy of Shadwell and Etheredge, would hardly commend themselves to one who had written verses for Shakespeare and may have known Ben Jonson. Further, it is clear that to Milton the whole of the English romantic drama, illumined by Shakespeare and Ben Jonson though it was, was conceived, *The Classic and Romantic Drama.* from a literary as well as an ethical point of view, on a wrong principle. With Sidney, he believed that the perfect drama was the Greek drama, and that the English stage, defying the unities, and mingling comedy with tragedy, had lost all proper sense of dramatic decorum. How contemptuously he dismisses 'common interludes' in the preface to *Samson Agonistes*! They undergo infamy "through the poet's error of intermixing comic stuff with tragic sadness and gravity; or introducing trivial and vulgar persons: which by all judicious hath been counted absurd, and brought in without discretion, corruptly to gratify the people". This criticism covers nearly every popular play, from Marlowe onwards; and yet another sin against Milton's literary canons had been committed by Dryden, who had deserted blank verse, and eked out his bombast with tags of heroic rhyme. In *Samson Agonistes*, then, Milton will not only scourge a backsliding age and foretell the vengeance to come; he will also show how a drama on the Greek lines and in the Greek spirit may be written in English blank verse. Of course, he was not the first to try such an experiment. The earlier

Elizabethan court-poets had revelled in such classical dramas as *Gorboduc* and *The Misfortunes of Arthur*, until Marlowe snuffed them out. At a later period, Daniel, in his *Philotas* and his *Cleopatra*, had attempted to renew the battle. But there is this very vital difference between Milton and his predecessors, that whereas they sought their inspiration in the frigid Latin imitations ascribed, probably in error, to the philosopher Seneca of Cordova, he went straight to the fountain-head and took as his models the three great masters of the Attic stage, Æschylus, Sophocles, and Euripides themselves. This, and Milton's genius, are the causes why, with the exception of a few works of our own day, such as Matthew Arnold's *Merope* and Swinburne's *Atalanta in Calydon*, *Samson Agonistes* stands alone as a literary achievement, and is the chief means whereby those ignorant of Greek can obtain some faint notion of what Athenian tragedy really was.

Greek tragedy arose out of ritual, out of the hymns sung by a band or chorus of worshippers as they danced around The Greek Drama. the altar of Dionysus. It became customary to vary the ceremony with the recital in monologue of legends wherein the god had played a part. In these hymns and this recital we find the germ of the two elements of the Greek drama as we know it, the dialogue and the choruses. A second and even a third speaker were gradually added to the original reciter: monologue gave way to dialogue; what was once narrated was now acted before the spectators. Thus the balance of interest shifted from the hymns to the legends presented between them, which were no longer concerned solely with Dionysus: but the chorus never disappeared and the religious character of the whole performance was never entirely forgotten. The chorus occupied the level floor of the theatre, known as the orchestra; in the centre was an altar, around which they moved in rhythmical evolutions when they were singing, at other times stood grouped in silence, their leader only taking part in the dialogue. On three sides of them were the semicircular tiers of spectators, on the fourth stood a narrow slightly raised stage for the actors, of whom never more than three, and in earlier days only two appeared at once. The scene was generally an open space before some building. The structure of the plays followed strictly conventional lines. First came the *Prologos*, during which one of the actors narrated the events which had led up to the beginning of the action. Then came the *Parodos*, with which the chorus filed singing into the orchestra. Then the action was developed in six scenes, of which the last was known as the *Exodos*, the other five as *Epeisodia*. Each *Epeisodion* was followed by a *Stasimon*, or song from the chorus. The dialogue was invariably in iambic verse; the *Stasima* and any incidental portions of song inserted into the *Epeisodia* were in various lyric metres. There was no possibility of shifting the scene, as the actors had to remain in sight of the audience throughout: hence the action had to be continuous in time and carried on in one spot from beginning to end. These limitations constitute the well-known classical unities of place and time. They are really subordinate to the more important unity of action, a principle that the action must contain the beginning, middle, and end of a single event, and nothing which does not form part of that event. It need hardly be said that comic elements were almost entirely excluded from strict tragedy. So much for the form of classical drama. With regard to the spirit it may be said: firstly, that it was essentially religious, much occupied with the ways of the gods and with their interference in human concerns. Secondly, that it was rhetorical, given to argument and to the utterance of wisdom in the form of gnomes or maxims. Thirdly, that it was serene, actual violence not being permitted on the stage, but, if it was necessary to the catastrophe, being reported by a messenger. Fourthly, that it was ironical, full of sentences of which the real meaning was only made clear by the event. Of course, the point of such irony depended upon the knowledge by the audience of what was going to happen and was as yet hidden from the actors. This knowledge was secured by the fact that the plot was always taken from some legend

thoroughly familiar to an Athenian audience. The part
played by the chorus was also peculiarly characteristic. In
the palmy days of the drama, that is to say, in Æschylus and
Sophocles, the themes of their odes are always connected
with the action: they even take a certain share in the action
itself. But it is generally a minor one. Their chief function
is to comment upon what happens, and to sympathize with
the principal actors. They give the counsels of moderation
and point the obvious morals. In a sense they may be said
to mediate between performers and spectators. They have
been called the ideal spectator. They indicate the attitude
which the poet wishes his play to suggest, voice the emotions
he would fain arouse. Such, then, were the form and the
spirit of Greek tragedy; the one is conscientiously reproduced,

Samson the other marvellously caught, in *Samson*
Agonistes *Agonistes*. Almost every point in the above
modelled on the
Greek Drama. necessarily brief summary might be illustrated
from the play. There are religion, maxims, serenity, irony
in abundance. The formal structure of *Prologos*, *Parodos*,
Epeisodia, *Stasima*, *Exodos* is preserved. So, too, are the
unities. The chorus plays its traditional *rôle*; the use of the
messenger is not forgotten. We cannot, I think, say that
Milton has made any one of the three great Attic tragedians
exclusively his model; he repeats certain traits of each. On
the whole, perhaps, he stands nearest to Sophocles. The
ethical tone, laying stress rather on free-will than on either
fate or accident as the motive cause of the tragedy; and the
tendency to rely for æsthetic effect rather upon structure than
upon graces of verbal ornament; both of these are less
Æschylean or Euripidean than Sophoclean. Yet to Euripides Milton must owe the exaggerated prolixity of argument, no less than the structure of what he calls the
'allaeostrophic' choruses: while something in the simplicity
of the story, in the majestic figure of the fettered Samson
resting on his bank and receiving in turn the visits of friends
and foes, forcibly recalls the very similar design of Æschylus'
Prometheus Vinctus.

Much of the interest of *Samson Agonistes* is due to the two points on which stress has been laid in this Introduction. It impresses us as a magnificent translation into English of the form and spirit of Greek tragedy, and it moves us as the record, full charged with pathos, of Milton's own sufferings and regrets. Either of these characteristics, and especially the latter, would suffice to make it a great poem. It cannot go for nothing in our judgment of a literary work that it is the intimate revelation of a marvellous personality. When Milton speaks his last word to the age, we, to some extent, waive our critic's right. Nevertheless it must be admitted that, viewed merely by itself, and apart from all relation to the writer or his time, the drama is lacking in some of the qualities which a good drama should have. This has been felt by many, and is admirably put by Mark Pattison.

Literary Merit of Samson Agonistes.

"The drama is languid, nerveless, occasionally halting, never brilliant. If the date of the composition of the *Samson* be 1663, this may have been the result of weariness after the effort of *Paradise Lost*. If this drama were composed in 1667, it would be the author's last poetical effort, and the natural explanation would then be that his power over language was failing. The power of metaphor, *i.e.* of indirect expression, is, according to Aristotle, the characteristic of genius. It springs from vividness of conception of the thing spoken of. It is evident that this intense action of the presentative faculty is no longer at the disposal of the writer of *Samson*. In *Paradise Regained* we are conscious of a purposed restraint of strength. The simplicity of its style is an experiment, an essay of a new theory of poetic words. The simplicity of *Samson Agonistes* is a flagging of the forces, a drying up of the rich sources from which had once flowed the golden stream of suggestive phrase which makes *Paradise Lost* a unique monument of the English language. I could almost fancy that the consciousness of decay utters itself in the lines—

'I feel my genial spirits droop,
My hopes all flat; Nature within me seems
In all her functions weary of herself;
My race of glory run, and race of shame,
And I shall shortly be with them that rest'."

On the whole, I think we must assent in the main to Mark Pattison's verdict on this point, although a question might be raised whether, in *Samson Agonistes* as well as in *Paradise Regained*, there is not something of 'purposed restraint', the less ornate style seeming to Milton the appropriate one for a drama on classical lines, since upon the Attic stage beauty of structure always went for more than beauty of decoration. Yet even when full allowance has been made for this, one cannot but still feel that *Samson Agonistes* is the work of an old, a world-wearied, an exhausted man. And indeed the structure shows no less signs of weakness than the diction. The plot lags lamentably, unfolds itself tediously. The opening part is intolerably prolix; the retrospection, which a Greek writer would have confined to a brief prologue, spreads itself over a waste of lines. And the two long interviews with Dalila and Harapha which follow advance the action but little. The sinuous wheedlings and triumphant jeers of the one, the insulting "bulk without spirit vast" of the other, serve doubtless to work Samson up to the strenuous pitch necessary for his great enterprise. But apart from this the scenes are episodes merely; they do not help to bring about the catastrophe; the summons of the Philistian lords might have been sent of their own motion without any incitement from Harapha. The lyrics of the choruses again, musical though they are in a subtle difficult fashion of their own, are not so infallibly musical as they should be, coming from the poet of the *Paradise Lost*. Milton has sought in them to reproduce the effect rather than the metres of the Greek choruses; to admit just the necessary variations from his blank-verse rhythms which would yield a lyrical note without loss of stateliness: but the experiment is not a perfectly successful one, and it is one which his earlier and undulled ear would probably not have made. And so throughout the play we have a sense of failing energies, of a Pegasus that answers more and more reluctantly to the spur, of a great design from which the inspiration has somehow unaccountably vanished, until just at the close the ancient fires are suddenly renewed, and the veteran poet takes his leave of us in some of the greatest, most majestic lines that the English language has ever endured:—

> "Come, come; no time for lamentation now,
> Nor much more cause: Samson hath quit himself

> Like Samson, and heroically hath finished
> A life heroic, on his enemies
> Fully revenged ; hath left them years of mourning,
> And lamentation to the sons of Caphtor
> Through all Philistian bounds : . . .
> Nothing is here for tears, nothing to wail
> Or knock the breast ; no weakness, no contempt,
> Dispraise, or blame ; nothing but well and fair,
> And what may quiet us in a death so noble."

These are the indomitable last words of an unquenchable spirit.

It is not necessary to make any elaborate search for the sources of *Samson Agonistes*. The action, that is, the catastrophe, is taken from the Book of *Judges*, chap. xvi., verses 23–30. And the allusions to Samson's past history are based upon chapters xiii.–xvi. of the same book. In the actual setting of the drama, the introduction of Dalila, of Manoa, and of Harapha, who does not really belong to the story at all, Milton has of course indulged his own imagination. But he has nowhere exceeded the probability of things. He may also have taken a hint or two from the *Antiquities* of Josephus, bk. v. chap. 8, and, according to Mr. Verity, may have consulted the account of the ruins of Gaza in the *Travels* of George Sandys. He does not seem to have borrowed anything from Quarles' *Historie of Samson* (1632), or from Alessandro Roselli's *Rappresentazione di Samsone* (1554), or from the anonymous French play on the subject printed in 1622. It is improbable that he ever heard of the Elizabethan play of *Samson* (circ. 1602), as this was never printed. Mr. Edmundson, in his *Milton and Vondel* (1885), has tried to show that Milton owed much to a drama by the Dutch poet Vondel, also on Samson (1660), and also cast in the classical form. The student will find an excellent analysis of Mr. Edmundson's ingenious but unconvincing arguments in Mr. Verity's admirable edition of *Samson Agonistes*.

OF THAT SORT OF DRAMATIC POEM

CALLED

TRAGEDY

Tragedy, as it was anciently composed, hath been ever held the gravest, moralest, and most profitable of all other poems: therefore said by Aristotle to be of power by raising pity and fear, or terror, to purge the mind of those and
5 such like passions; that is, to temper and reduce them to just measure with a kind of delight, stirred up by reading or seeing those passions well imitated. Nor is Nature wanting in her own effects to make good his assertion; for so in physic things of melancholy hue and quality are used
10 against melancholy, sour against sour, salt to remove salt humours. Hence philosophers and other gravest writers, as Cicero, Plutarch, and others, frequently cite out of tragic poets, both to adorn and illustrate their discourse. The apostle Paul himself thought it not unworthy to insert a
15 verse of Euripides into the text of Holy Scripture, *1 Cor.* xv. 33; and Paraeus, commenting on the *Revelation*, divides the whole book as a tragedy, into acts, distinguished each by a Chorus of heavenly harpings and song between. Heretofore men in highest dignity have laboured not a little to
20 be thought able to compose a tragedy. Of that honour Dionysius the elder was no less ambitious, than before of his attaining to the tyranny. Augustus Caesar also had begun his *Ajax*, but unable to please his own judgment with what he had begun, left it unfinished. Seneca the philosopher
25 is by some thought the author of those tragedies (at least the best of them) that go under that name. Gregory Nazianzen, a Father of the Church, thought it not unbeseeming the sanctity of his person to write a tragedy, which he entitled *Christ Suffering*. This is mentioned to vindicate

26

tragedy from the small esteem, or rather infamy, which in
the account of many it undergoes at this day with other
common interludes; happening through the poet's error of
intermixing comic stuff with tragic sadness and gravity;
or introducing trivial and vulgar persons: which by all judicious hath been counted absurd, and brought in without
discretion, corruptly to gratify the people. And though
ancient tragedy use no Prologue, yet using sometimes, in
case of self-defence, or explanation, that which Martial
calls an Epistle; in behalf of this tragedy coming forth
after the ancient manner, much different from what among
us passes for best, thus much beforehand may be epistled;
that Chorus is here introduced after the Greek manner, not
ancient only but modern, and still in use among the Italians.
In the modelling therefore of this poem, with good reason,
the Ancients and Italians are rather followed, as of much
more authority and fame. The measure of verse used in
the Chorus is of all sorts, called by the Greeks Monostro-
phic, or rather Apolelymenon, without regard had to Strophe,
Antistrophe, or Epode, which were a kind of stanzas framed
only for the music, then used with the Chorus that sung;
not essential to the poem, and therefore not material: or
being divided into stanzas or pauses, they may be called
Allaeostropha. Division into Act and Scene referring chiefly
to the stage (to which this work never was intended) is here
omitted.

It suffices if the whole drama be found not produced
beyond the fifth act. Of the style and uniformity, and that
commonly called the plot, whether intricate or explicit,
which is nothing indeed but such economy or disposition
of the fable as may stand best with verisimilitude and
decorum, they only will best judge who are not unac-
quainted with Aeschylus, Sophocles, and Euripides, the
three tragic poets unequalled yet by any, and the best rule
to all who endeavour to write tragedy. The circumscrip-
tion of time wherein the whole drama begins and ends, is,
according to ancient rule, and best example, within the
space of twenty-four hours.

THE ARGUMENT

Samson, made captive, blind, and now in the prison at Gaza, there to labour as in a common workhouse, on a festival day, in the general cessation from labour, comes forth into the open air, to a place nigh, somewhat retired, there to sit awhile and bemoan his condition. Where he happens at length to be visited by certain friends and equals of his tribe, which make the Chorus, who seek to comfort him what they can; then by his old father, Manoa, who endeavours the like, and withal tells him his purpose to procure his liberty by ransom; lastly, that this feast was proclaimed by the Philistines as a day of thanksgiving for their deliverance from the hands of Samson, which yet more troubles him. Manoa then departs to prosecute his endeavour with the Philistian lords for Samson's redemption; who in the meanwhile is visited by other persons; and lastly by a public officer to require his coming to the feast before the lords and people, to play or show his strength in their presence. He at first refuses, dismissing the public officer with absolute denial to come; at length persuaded inwardly that this was from God, he yields to go along with him, who came now the second time with great threatenings to fetch him. The Chorus yet remaining on the place, Manoa returns full of joyful hope, to procure ere long his son's deliverance: in the midst of which discourse an Ebrew comes in haste, confusedly at first, and afterwards more distinctly, relating the catastrophe, what Samson had done to the Philistines, and by accident to himself; wherewith the Tragedy ends.

SAMSON AGONISTES

THE PERSONS

SAMSON.
MANOA, *the Father of Samson.*
DALILA, *his Wife.*
HARAPHA *of Gath.*
Public Officer.
Messenger.
Chorus of Danites.

The Scene, before the prison in Gaza

SAMSON

A little onward lend thy guiding hand
To these dark steps, a little further on;
For yonder bank hath choice of sun or shade;
There I am wont to sit, when any chance
Relieves me from my task of servile toil,   5
Daily in the common prison else enjoin'd me;
Where I, a prisoner chain'd, scarce freely draw
The air imprison'd also, close and damp,
Unwholesome draught.   But here I feel amends,
The breath of heaven fresh-blowing, pure and sweet,   10
With day-spring born; here leave me to respire.
This day a solemn feast the people hold
To Dagon, their sea-idol, and forbid
Laborious works; unwillingly this rest
Their superstition yields me; hence, with leave   15
Retiring from the popular noise, I seek
This unfrequented place to find some ease;
Ease to the body some, none to the mind
From restless thoughts, that, like a deadly swarm
Of hornets arm'd, no sooner found alone,   20
But rush upon me thronging, and present

Times past, what once I was, and what am now.
O wherefore was my birth from Heaven foretold
Twice by an Angel, who at last, in sight
Of both my parents, all in flames ascended   25
From off the altar, where an offering burn'd,
As in a fiery column charioting
His god-like presence, and from some great act
Or benefit reveal'd to Abraham's race?
Why was my breeding order'd and prescribed   30
As of a person separate to God,
Design'd for great exploits; if I must die
Betray'd, captived, and both my eyes put out,
Made of my enemies the scorn and gaze,
To grind in brazen fetters under task   35
With this Heaven-gifted strength? O glorious strength,
Put to the labour of a beast, debased
Lower than bond-slave! Promise was that I
Should Israel from Philistian yoke deliver;
Ask for this great deliverer now, and find him   40
Eyeless, in Gaza, at the mill, with slaves,
Himself in bonds under Philistian yoke.
Yet stay; let me not rashly call in doubt
Divine prediction; what if all foretold
Had been fulfill'd but through mine own default?   45
Whom have I to complain of but myself?
Who this high gift of strength committed to me,
In what part lodged, how easily bereft me,
Under the seal of silence could not keep,
But weakly to a woman must reveal it,   50
O'ercome with importunity and tears.
O impotence of mind in body strong!
But what is strength, without a double share
Of wisdom? Vast, unwieldy, burdensome,
Proudly secure, yet liable to fall   55
By weakest subtleties; not made to rule,
But to subserve where wisdom bears command.
God, when he gave me strength, to show withal
How slight the gift was, hung it in my hair.

But peace!   I must not quarrel with the will   60
Of highest dispensation, which herein
Haply had ends above my reach to know.
Suffices that to me strength is my bane,
And proves the source of all my miseries,
So many, and so huge, that each apart   65
Would ask a life to wail.   But chief of all,
O loss of sight, of thee I most complain!
Blind among enemies!   O worse than chains,
Dungeon, or beggary, or decrepit age!
Light, the prime work of God, to me is extinct,   70
And all her various objects of delight
Annull'd, which might in part my grief have eased,
Inferior to the vilest now become
Of man or worm; the vilest here excel me:
They creep, yet see; I, dark in light, exposed   75
To daily fraud, contempt, abuse and wrong,
Within doors, or without, still as a fool,
In power of others, never in my own,
Scarce half I seem to live, dead more than half
O dark, dark, dark, amid the blaze of noon,   80
Irrecoverably dark, total eclipse
Without all hope of day!
O first-created beam, and thou great Word,
' Let there be light, and light was over all ',
Why am I thus bereaved thy prime decree?   85
The Sun to me is dark
And silent as the Moon
When she deserts the night,
Hid in her vacant interlunar cave.
Since light so necessary is to life,   90
And almost life itself, if it be true
That light is in the soul,
She all in every part; why was the sight
To such a tender ball as the eye confined,
So obvious and so easy to be quench'd?   95
And not, as feeling, through all parts diffused,
That she might look at will through every pore?

Then had I not been thus exiled from light
As in the land of darkness, yet in light
To live a life half dead, a living death,   100
And buried; but (O yet more miserable!)
Myself my sepulchre, a moving grave.
Buried, yet not exempt
By privilege of death and burial
From worst of other evils, pains and wrongs;   105
But made hereby obnoxious more
To all the miseries of life,
Life in captivity
Among inhuman foes.
But who are these? for with joint pace I hear   110
The tread of many feet steering this way;
Perhaps my enemies, who come to stare
At my affliction, and perhaps to insult—
Their daily practice to afflict me more.

CHORUS.

 Chorus. This, this is he; softly awhile;   115
Let us not break in upon him.
O change beyond report, thought, or belief!
See how he lies at random, carelessly diffused,
With languish'd head unpropp'd,
As one past hope, abandon'd,   120
And by himself given over;
In slavish habit, ill-fitted weeds
O'er-worn and soil'd.
Or do my eyes misrepresent? Can this be he,
That heroic, that renown'd,   125
Irresistible Samson? whom unarm'd
No strength of man, or fiercest wild beast, could withstand;
Who tore the lion, as the lion tears the kid;
Ran on embattled armies clad in iron,
And weaponless himself,   130
Made arms ridiculous, useless the forgery
Of brazen shield and spear, the hammer'd cuirass,
Chalybean-temper'd steel, and frock of mail

Adamantean proof:
But safest he who stood aloof,   135
When insupportably his foot advanced,
In scorn of their proud arms and warlike tools,
Spurn'd them to death by troops.   The bold Ascalonite
Fled from his lion ramp, old warriors turn'd
Their plated backs under his heel;   140
Or groveling soil'd their crested helmets in the dust.
Then with what trivial weapon came to hand,
The jaw of a dead ass, his sword of bone,
A thousand foreskins fell, the flower of Palestine,
In Ramath-lechi, famous to this day: 145
Then by main force pull'd up, and on his shoulders bore
The gates of Azza, post and massy bar,
Up to the hill by Hebron, seat of giants old—
No journey of a Sabbath-day, and loaded so—
Like whom the Gentiles feign to bear up Heaven.   150
Which shall I first bewail,
Thy bondage or lost sight,
Prison within prison
Inseparably dark?
Thou art become (O worst imprisonment!)   155
The dungeon of thyself; thy soul
(Which men enjoying sight oft without cause complain)
Imprison'd now indeed,
In real darkness of the body dwells,
Shut up from outward light   160
To incorporate with gloomy night;
For inward light, alas!
Puts forth no visual beam.
O mirror of our fickle state,
Since man on earth, unparallel'd!   165
The rarer thy example stands,
By how much from the top of wondrous glory,
Strongest of mortal men,
To lowest pitch of abject fortune thou art fall'n.
For him I reckon not in high estate   170
Whom long descent of birth
(M 380)   B

Or the sphere of fortune raises;
But thee, whose strength, while virtue was her mate,
Might have subdued the Earth,
Universally crown'd with highest praises.   175
   Samson. I hear the sound of words; their sense the air
Dissolves unjointed ere it reach my ear.
   Chorus. He speaks; let us draw nigh. Matchless in might,
The glory late of Israel, now the grief!
We come, thy friends and neighbours not unknown,   180
From Eshtaol and Zora's fruitful vale,
To visit or bewail thee; or, if better,
Counsel or consolation we may bring,
Salve to thy sores; apt words have power to suage
The tumours of a troubled mind,   185
And are as balm to fester'd wounds.
   Samson. Your coming, friends, revives me; for I learn
Now of my own experience, not by talk,
How counterfeit a coin they are who 'friends'
Bear in their superscription (of the most   190
I would be understood). In prosperous days
They swarm, but in adverse withdraw their head,
Not to be found, though sought. Ye see, O friends,
How many evils have enclosed me round;
Yet that which was the worst now least afflicts me,   195
Blindness; for had I sight, confused with shame,
How could I once look up, or heave the head,
Who, like a foolish pilot, have shipwrack'd
My vessel trusted to me from above,
Gloriously rigg'd, and for a word, a tear,   200
Fool! have divulged the secret gift of God
To a deceitful woman? Tell me, friends,
Am I not sung and proverb'd for a fool
In every street? Do they not say, 'How well
Are come upon him his deserts'? Yet why?   205
Immeasurable strength they might behold
In me; of wisdom nothing more than mean.
This with the other should, at least, have pair'd;
These two, proportion'd ill, drove me transverse.

Chorus. Tax not divine disposal. Wisest men   210
Have err'd, and by bad women been deceived;
And shall again, pretend they ne'er so wise.
Deject not, then, so overmuch thyself,
Who hast of sorrow thy full load besides.
Yet, truth to say, I oft have heard men wonder   215
Why thou should'st wed Philistian women rather
Than of thine own tribe fairer, or as fair,
At least of thy own nation, and as noble.

Samson. The first I saw at Timna, and she pleased
Me, not my parents, that I sought to wed   220
The daughter of an infidel: they knew not
That what I motion'd was of God; I knew
From intimate impulse, and therefore urged
The marriage on, that by occasion hence
I might begin Israel's deliverance,   225
The work to which I was divinely call'd.
She proving false, the next I took to wife
(O that I never had! fond wish too late!)
Was in the vale of Sorec, Dalila,
That specious monster, my accomplish'd snare.   230
I thought it lawful from my former act,
And the same end, still watching to oppress
Israel's oppressors. Of what now I suffer
She was not the prime cause, but I myself;
Who, vanquish'd with a peal of words (O weakness!),   235
Gave up my fort of silence to a woman.

Chorus. In seeking just occasion to provoke
The Philistine, thy country's enemy,
Thou never wast remiss, I bear thee witness:
Yet Israel still serves with all his sons.   240

Samson. That fault I take not on me, but transfer
On Israel's governors and heads of tribes,
Who seeing those great acts which God had done
Singly by me against their conquerors,
Acknowledged not, or not at all consider'd   245
Deliverance offer'd. I on the other side
Used no ambition to commend my deeds;

The deeds themselves, though mute, spoke loud the doer
But they persisted deaf, and would not seem
To count them things worth notice, till at length   250
Their lords, the Philistines, with gather'd powers
Enter'd Judea, seeking me, who then
Safe to the rock of Etham was retired,
Not flying, but fore-casting in what place
To set upon them, what advantaged best.   255
Meanwhile the men of Judah, to prevent
The harass of their land, beset me round;
I willingly on some conditions came
Into their hands, and they as gladly yield me
To the Uncircumcised a welcome prey,   260
Bound with two cords.   But cords to me were threads
Touch'd with the flame: on their whole host I flew
Unarm'd, and with a trivial weapon fell'd
Their choicest youth; they only lived who fled.
Had Judah that day join'd, or one whole tribe,   265
They had by this possess'd the towers of Gath,
And lorded over them whom they now serve.
But what more oft in nations grown corrupt,
And by their vices brought to servitude,
Than to love bondage more than liberty,   270
Bondage with ease than strenuous liberty;
And to despise, or envy, or suspect
Whom God hath of his special favour raised
As their deliverer? If he aught begin,
How frequent to desert him, and at last   275
To heap ingratitude on worthiest deeds!
    Chorus. Thy words to my remembrance bring
How Succoth and the fort of Penuel
Their great deliverer contemn'd,
The matchless Gideon in pursuit   280
Of Madian and her vanquish'd kings:
And how ingrateful Ephraim
Had dealt with Jephtha, who by argument,
Not worse than by his shield and spear,
Defended Israel from the Ammonite,   285

Had not his prowess quell'd their pride
In that sore battle when so many died
Without reprieve, adjudged to death,
For want of well pronouncing *Shibboleth*.

    Samson. Of such examples add me to the roll;   290
Me easily indeed mine may neglect,
But God's proposed deliverance not so.

    Chorus. Just are the ways of God,
And justifiable to men;
Unless there be who think not God at all: 295
If any be, they walk obscure;
For of such doctrine never was there school,
But the heart of the fool,
And no man therein doctor but himself.

    Yet more there be who doubt his ways not just,   300
As to his own edicts found contradicting;
Then give the reins to wandering thought,
Regardless of his glory's diminution,
Till, by their own perplexities involved,
They ravel more, still less resolved,   305
But never find self-satisfying solution.

    As if they would confine the Interminable,
And tie him to his own prescript,
Who made our laws to bind us, not himself,
And hath full right to exempt   310
Whomso it pleases him by choice
From national obstriction, without taint
Of sin, or legal debt;
For with his own laws he can best dispense.

    He would not else, who never wanted means,   315
Nor in respect of the enemy just cause,
To set his people free,
Have prompted this heroic Nazarite,
Against his vow of strictest purity,
To seek in marriage that fallacious bride,   320
Unclean, unchaste.

    Down, Reason, then; at least, vain reasonings down;
Though Reason here aver

That moral verdict quits her of unclean:
Unchaste was subsequent; her stain, not his.   325
    But see! here comes thy reverend sire,
With careful step, locks white as down,
Old Manoa: advise
Forthwith how thou ought'st to receive him.
    Samson. Ay me, another inward grief, awaked   330
With mention of that name, renews the assault.

MANOA.

    Manoa. Brethren and men of Dan (for such ye seem,
Though in this uncouth place), if old respect,
As I suppose, towards your once gloried friend,
My son, now captive, hither hath inform'd   335
Your younger feet, while mine, cast back with age,
Came lagging after, say if he be here.
    Chorus. As signal now in low dejected state,
As erst in highest, behold him where he lies.
    Manoa. O miserable change! Is this the man,   340
That invincible Samson, far renown'd,
The dread of Israel's foes, who with a strength
Equivalent to angels' walk'd their streets,
None offering fight; who, single combatant,
Duell'd their armies rank'd in proud array,   345
Himself an army—now unequal match
To save himself against a coward arm'd
At one spear's length? O ever-failing trust
In mortal strength! and, oh, what not in man
Deceivable and vain! nay, what thing good   350
Pray'd for, but often proves our woe, our bane?
I pray'd for children, and thought barrenness
In wedlock a reproach; I gain'd a son,
And such a son as all men hail'd me happy:
Who would be now a father in my stead?   355
O wherefore did God grant me my request,
And as a blessing with such pomp adorn'd?
Why are his gifts desirable, to tempt
Our earnest prayers—then, given with solemn hand

As graces, draw a scorpion's tail behind?   360
For this did the Angel twice descend? for this
Ordain'd thy nurture holy, as of a plant
Select and sacred? glorious for a while,
The miracle of men: then in an hour
Ensnared, assaulted, overcome, led bound,   365
Thy foes' derision, captive, poor, and blind,
Into a dungeon thrust, to work with slaves!
Alas! methinks whom God hath chosen once
To worthiest deeds, if he through frailty err,
He should not so o'erwhelm, and as a thrall,   370
Subject him to so foul indignities,
Be it but for honour's sake of former deeds.
    Samson. Appoint not heavenly disposition, father.
Nothing of all these evils hath befall'n me
But justly; I myself have brought them on,   375
Sole author I, sole cause: if aught seem vile,
As vile hath been my folly, who have profaned
The mystery of God, giv'n me under pledge
Of vow, and have betray'd it to a woman,
A Canaanite, my faithless enemy.   380
This well I knew, nor was at all surprised,
But warn'd by oft experience. Did not she
Of Timna first betray me, and reveal
The secret wrested from me in her highth
Of nuptial love profess'd, carrying it straight   385
To them who had corrupted her, my spies
And rivals? In this other was there found
More faith? who also in her prime of love,
Spousal embraces, vitiated with gold,
Though offer'd only, by the scent conceived   390
Her spurious first-born, Treason against me.
Thrice she assay'd, with flattering prayers and sighs,
And amorous reproaches, to win from me
My capital secret, in what part my strength
Lay stored, in what part summ'd, that she might know;   395
Thrice I deluded her, and turned to sport
Her importunity, each time perceiving

How openly and with what impudence
She purposed to betray me; and (which was worse
Than undissembled hate) with what contempt   400
She sought to make me traitor to myself.
Yet the fourth time, when mustering all her wiles,
With blandish'd parleys, feminine assaults,
Tongue-batteries, she surceased not day nor night
To storm me over-watch'd, and wearied out,   405
At times when men seek most repose and rest,
I yielded, and unlock'd her all my heart;
Who, with a grain of manhood well resolved,
Might easily have shook off all her snares:
But foul effeminacy held me yoked   410
Her bond-slave. O indignity, O blot
To honour and religion! servile mind,
Rewarded well with servile punishment!
The base degree to which I now am fall'n,
These rags, this grinding, is not yet so base   415
As was my former servitude, ignoble,
Unmanly, ignominious, infamous,
True slavery, and that blindness worse than this,
That saw not how degenerately I served.
    Manoa. I cannot praise thy marriage-choices, son,   420
Rather approved them not; but thou didst plead
Divine impulsion prompting how thou mightst
Find some occasion to infest our foes.
I state not that; this I am sure—our foes
Found soon occasion thereby to make thee   425
Their captive, and their triumph; thou the sooner
Temptation found'st, or over-potent charms
To violate the sacred trust of silence
Deposited within thee; which to have kept
Tacit, was in thy power. True; and thou bear'st   430
Enough, and more, the burden of that fault;
Bitterly hast thou paid, and still art paying
That rigid score. A worse thing yet remains;
This day the Philistines a popular feast
Here celebrate in Gaza, and proclaim   435

Imp[?] ... [?]
thing to
spur Samson
on to revenge.

Great pomp, and sacrifice, and praises loud
To Dagon, as their god who hath deliver'd
Thee, Samson, bound and blind, into their hands—
Them out of thine, who slew'st them many a slain.
So Dagon shall be magnified, and God,   440
Besides whom is no God, compared with idols,
Disglorified, blasphemed, and had in scorn
By the idolatrous rout amidst their wine;
Which to have come to pass by means of thee,
Samson, of all thy sufferings think the heaviest,   445
Of all reproach the most with shame that ever
Could have befall'n thee and thy father's house.
  Samson. Father, I do acknowledge and confess
That I this honour, I this pomp have brought
To Dagon, and advanced his praises high   450
Among the heathen round; to God have brought
Dishonour, obloquy, and oped the mouths
Of idolists and atheists; have brought scandal
To Israel, diffidence of God, and doubt
In feeble hearts, propense enough before   455
To waver, or fall off and join with idols;
Which is my chief affliction, shame and sorrow,
The anguish of my soul, that suffers not
Mine eye to harbour sleep, or thoughts to rest.
This only hope relieves me, that the strife   460
With me hath end; all the contest is now
'Twixt God and Dagon. Dagon hath presumed,
Me overthrown, to enter lists with God,
His deity comparing and preferring
Before the God of Abraham. He, be sure,   465
Will not connive, or linger, thus provoked,
But will arise, and his great name assert:
Dagon must stoop, and shall ere long receive
Such a discomfit, as shall quite despoil him
Of all these boasted trophies won on me,   470
And with confusion blank his worshippers.
  Man. With cause this hope relieves thee; and these words
I as a prophecy receive; for God

(Nothing more certain) will not long defer
To vindicate the glory of his name   475
Against all competition, nor will long
Endure it doubtful whether God be Lord,
Or Dagon.   But for thee what shall be done?
Thou must not in the meanwhile, here forgot,
Lie in this miserable loathsome plight,   480
Neglected.   I already have made way
To some Philistian lords, with whom to treat
About thy ransom.   Well they may by this
Have satisfied their utmost of revenge
By pains and slaveries, worse than death, inflicted   485
On thee, who now no more canst do them harm.
   Samson.   Spare that proposal, father, spare the trouble
Of that solicitation; let me here,
As I deserve, pay on my punishment,
And expiate, if possible, my crime,   490
Shameful garrulity.   To have reveal'd
Secrets of men, the secrets of a friend,
How heinous had the fact been, how deserving
Contempt, and scorn of all—to be excluded
All friendship, and avoided as a blab,   495
The mark of fool set on his front!   But I
God's counsel have not kept, his holy secret
Presumptuously have publish'd, impiously,
Weakly at least, and shamefully; a sin
That Gentiles in their parables condemn   500
To their Abyss and horrid pains confined.
   Manoa.   Be penitent, and for thy fault contrite,
But act not in thy own affliction, son:
Repent the sin, but if the punishment
Thou canst avoid, self-preservation bids;   505
Or the execution leave to high disposal,
And let another hand, not thine, exact
Thy penal forfeit from thyself.   Perhaps
God will relent, and quit thee all his debt;
Who ever more approves and more accepts   510
(Best pleased with humble and filial submission)

Him who, imploring mercy, sues for life,
Than who, self-rigorous, chooses death as due;
Which argues over-just, and self-displeased,
For self-offence, more than for God offended.   515
Reject not, then, what offer'd means who knows
But God hath set before us to return thee
Home to thy country and his sacred house,
Where thou mayst bring thy offerings, to avert
His further ire, with prayers and vows renew'd.   520
   Samson. His pardon I implore; but as for life,
To what end should I seek it? When in strength
All mortals I excell'd, and great in hopes,
With youthful courage and magnanimous thoughts
Of birth from Heaven foretold and high exploits,   525
Full of divine instinct, after some proof
Of acts indeed heroic, far beyond
The sons of Anak, famous now and blazed,
Fearless of danger, like a petty god
I walked about, admired of all, and dreaded   530
On hostile ground, none daring my affront.
Then, swoll'n with pride, into the snare I fell
Of fair, fallacious looks, venereal trains,
Soften'd with pleasure and voluptuous life,
At length to lay my head and hallow'd pledge   535
Of all my strength in the lascivious lap
Of a deceitful concubine, who shore me,
Like a tame wether, all my precious fleece,
Then turn'd me out ridiculous, despoil'd,
Shav'n, and disarm'd among my enemies.   540
   Chorus. Desire of wine and all delicious drinks,
Which many a famous warrior overturns,
Thou couldst repress; nor did the dancing ruby,
Sparkling out-pour'd, the flavour, or the smell,
Or taste that cheers the heart of gods and men,   545
Allure thee from the cool crystalline stream.
   Samson. Wherever fountain or fresh current flow'd
Against the eastern ray, translucent, pure
With touch ethereal of Heaven's fiery rod,

I drank, from the clear milky juice allaying   550
Thirst, and refresh'd : nor envied them the grape
Whose heads that turbulent liquor fills with fumes.
   Chorus. O madness! to think use of strongest wines
And strongest drinks our chief support of health,
When God with these forbidd'n made choice to rear   555
His mighty champion, strong above compare,
Whose drink was only from the liquid brook!
   Samson. But what avail'd this temperance, not complete
Against another object more enticing?
What boots it at one gate to make defence,   560
And at another to let in the foe,
Effeminately vanquish'd? by which means,
Now blind, dishearten'd, shamed, dishonour'd, quell'd,
To what can I be useful? wherein serve
My nation, and the work from Heaven imposed?   565
But to sit idle on the household hearth,
A burdenous drone; to visitants a gaze,
Or pitied object; these redundant locks,
Robustious to no purpose, clustering down,
Vain monument of strength; till length of years   570
And sedentary numbness craze my limbs
To a contemptible old age obscure.
Here rather let me drudge, and earn my bread,
Till vermin, or the draff of servile food,
Consume me, and oft-invocated death   575
Hasten the welcome end of all my pains.
   Manoa. Wilt thou then serve the Philistines with that gift
Which was expressly given thee to annoy them?
Better at home lie bed-rid, not only idle,
Inglorious, unemploy'd, with age outworn.   580
But God, who caused a fountain at thy prayer
From the dry ground to spring, thy thirst to allay
After the brunt of battle, can as easy
Cause light again within thy eyes to spring,
Wherewith to serve him better than thou hast.   585
And I persuade me so: why else this strength
Miraculous yet remaining in those locks?

His might continues in thee not for naught,
Nor shall his wondrous gifts be frustrate thus.
   Samson. All otherwise to me my thoughts portend— 590
That these dark orbs no more shall treat with light,
Nor the other light of life continue long,
But yield to double darkness nigh at hand:
So much I feel my genial spirits droop,
My hopes all flat; Nature within me seems 595
In all her functions weary of herself;
My race of glory run, and race of shame,
And I shall shortly be with them that rest.
   Manoa. Believe not these suggestions, which proceed
From anguish of the mind and humours black 600
That mingle with thy fancy. I however
Must not omit a father's timely care
To prosecute the means of thy deliverance,
By ransom or how else: meanwhile be calm,
And healing words from these thy friends admit. [*Exit.* 605
   Samson. O that torment should not be confined
To the body's wounds and sores,
With maladies innumerable
In heart, head, breast, and reins;
But must secret passage find 610
To the inmost mind,
There exercise all his fierce accidents,
And on her purest spirits prey
As on entrails, joints, and limbs,
With answerable pains, but more intense, 615
Though void of corporal sense!
  My griefs not only pain me
As a lingering disease,
But, finding no redress, ferment and rage;
Nor less than wounds immedicable 620
Rankle, and fester, and gangrene,
To black mortification.
Thoughts my tormentors, arm'd with deadly stings,
Mangle my apprehensive tenderest parts;
Exasperate, exulcerate, and raise 625

Dire inflammation which no cooling herb
Or medicinal liquor can assuage,
Nor breath of vernal air from snowy Alp.
Sleep hath forsook and given me o'er
To death's benumbing opium as my only cure: 630
Thence faintings, swoonings of despair,
And sense of Heaven's desertion.
   I was his nursling once and choice delight,
His destined from the womb,
Promised by Heavenly message twice descending.   635
Under his special eye
Abstemious I grew up and thrived amain;
He led me on to mightiest deeds
Above the nerve of mortal arm,
Against the Uncircumcised, our enemies: 640
But now hath cast me off as never known,
And to those cruel enemies,
Whom I by his appointment had provoked,
Left me all helpless with the irreparable loss
Of sight, reserved alive to be repeated   645
The subject of their cruelty or scorn.
Nor am I in the list of them that hope;
Hopeless are all my evils, all remediless;
This one prayer yet remains, might I be heard,
No long petition—speedy death,   650
The close of all my miseries, and the balm.
   Chorus. Many are the sayings of the wise,
In ancient and in modern books enroll'd,
Extolling patience as the truest fortitude,
And to the bearing well of all calamities,   655
All chances incident to man's frail life,
Consolatories writ
With studied argument, and much persuasion sought,
Lenient of grief and anxious thought;
But with the afflicted in his pangs their sound   660
Little prevails, or rather seems a tune
Harsh, and of dissonant mood from his complaint,
Unless he feel within

Some source of consolation from above;
Secret refreshings that repair his strength,   665
And fainting spirits uphold.
   God of our fathers! what is Man,
That thou towards him with hand so various
(Or might I say contrarious?),
Temper'st thy providence through his short course,   670
Not evenly, as thou rulest
The angelic orders, and inferior creatures mute,
Irrational and brute?
Nor do I name of men the common rout,
That wandering loose about,   675
Grow up and perish as the summer-fly,
Heads without name, no more remembered;
But such as thou hast solemnly elected,
With gifts and graces eminently adorn'd
To some great work, thy glory,   680
And people's safety, which in part they effect:
Yet towards these thus dignified, thou oft
Amidst their highth of noon,
Changest thy countenance and thy hand, with no regard
Of highest favours past   685
From thee on them, or them to thee of service.
   Nor only dost degrade them, or remit
To life obscured, which were a fair dismission,
But throw'st them lower than thou didst exalt them high—
Unseemly falls in human eye,   690
Too grievous for the trespass or omission;
Oft leav'st them to the hostile sword
Of heathen and profane, their carcasses
To dogs and fowls a prey, or else captived;
Or to the unjust tribunals, under change of times,   695
And condemnation of the ungrateful multitude.
If these they scape, perhaps in poverty
With sickness and disease thou bow'st them down,
Painful diseases, and deform'd,
In crude old age;   700
Though not disordinate, yet causeless suffering

The punishment of dissolute days: in fine,
Just or unjust alike seem miserable,
For oft alike both come to evil end.
　　So deal not with this once thy glorious champion,　705
The image of thy strength, and mighty minister.
What do I beg? how hast thou dealt already!
Behold him in this state calamitous, and turn
His labours, for thou canst, to peaceful end.
　　But who is this, what thing of sea or land—　710
Female of sex it seems,—
That so bedeck'd, ornate, and gay,
Comes this way sailing
Like a stately ship
Of Tarsus, bound for the isles　715
Of Javan or Gadire,
With all her bravery on, and tackle trim,
Sails fill'd, and streamers waving,
Courted by all the winds that hold them play;
An amber scent of odorous perfume　720
Her harbinger, a damsel train behind?
Some rich Philistian matron she may seem;
And now, at nearer view, no other certain
Than Dalila, thy wife.　724
　　Samson. My wife! my traitress! let her not come near me.
　　Chorus. Yet on she moves; now stands, and eyes thee fix'd,
About to have spoke; but now, with head declined,
Like a fair flower surcharged with dew, she weeps,
And words address'd seem into tears dissolved,
Wetting the borders of her silken veil:　730
But now again she makes address to speak.

DALILA.

　　Dalila. With doubtful feet and wavering resolution
I came, still dreading thy displeasure, Samson,
Which to have merited, without excuse,
I cannot but acknowledge. Yet, if tears　735
May expiate (though the fact more evil drew
In the perverse event than I foresaw),

My penance hath not slacken'd, though my pardon
No way assured.   But conjugal affection,
Prevailing over fear and timorous doubt,   740
Hath led me on, desirous to behold
Once more thy face, and know of thy estate,
If aught in my ability may serve
To lighten what thou suffer'st, and appease
Thy mind with what amends is in my power—   745
Though late, yet in some part to recompense
My rash but more unfortunate misdeed.
   Samson. Out, out, hyaena!   These are thy wonted arts,
And arts of every woman false like thee,
To break all faith, all vows, deceive, betray;   750
Then, as repentant, to submit, beseech,
And reconcilement move with feign'd remorse,
Confess, and promise wonders in her change—
Not truly penitent, but chief to try
Her husband, how far urged his patience bears,   755
His virtue or weakness which way to assail:
Then with more cautious and instructed skill
Again transgresses, and again submits;
That wisest and best men, full oft beguiled,
With goodness principled not to reject   760
The penitent, but ever to forgive,
Are drawn to wear out miserable days,
Entangled with a poisonous bosom-snake,
If not by quick destruction soon cut off,
As I by thee, to ages an example.   765
   Dalila. Yet hear me, Samson; not that I endeavour
To lessen or extenuate my offence,
But that on the other side if it be weigh'd
By itself, with aggravations not surcharged,
Or else with just allowance counterpoised,   770
I may, if possible, thy pardon find
The easier towards me, or thy hatred less.
First granting, as I do, it was a weakness
In me, but incident to all our sex,
Curiosity, inquisitive, importune   775

Of secrets, then with like infirmity
To publish them—both common female faults:
Was it not weakness also to make known
For importunity, that is for naught,
Wherein consisted all thy strength and safety?   780
To what I did thou show'dst me first the way.
But I to enemies reveal'd, and should not!
Nor shouldst thou have trusted that to woman's frailty:
Ere I to thee, thou to thyself wast cruel.
Let weakness then with weakness come to parle,   785
So near related, or the same of kind;
Thine forgive mine; that men may censure thine
The gentler, if severely thou exact not
More strength from me than in thyself was found.
And what if love, which thou interpret'st hate,   790
The jealousy of love, powerful of sway
In human hearts, nor less in mine towards thee,
Caused what I did?   I saw thee mutable
Of fancy; fear'd lest one day thou would'st leave me
As her at Timna; sought by all means, therefore,   795
How to endear, and hold thee to me firmest:
No better way I saw than by importuning
To learn thy secrets, get into my power
Thy key of strength and safety.   Thou wilt say,
Why then reveal'd?   I was assured by those   800
Who tempted me, that nothing was design'd
Against thee but safe custody and hold:
That made for me; I knew that liberty
Would draw thee forth to perilous enterprises,
While I at home sat full of cares and fears,   805
Wailing thy absence in my widow'd bed;
Here I should still enjoy thee, day and night,
Mine and love's prisoner, not the Philistines',
Whole to myself, unhazarded abroad,
Fearless at home of partners in my love.   810
These reasons in love's law have pass'd for good,
Though fond and reasonless to some perhaps;
And love hath oft, well meaning, wrought much woe.

Yet always pity or pardon hath obtain'd.
Be not unlike all others, not austere   815
As thou art strong, inflexible as steel.
If thou in strength all mortals dost exceed,
In uncompassionate anger do not so.
   Samson. How cunningly the sorceress displays
Her own transgressions, to upbraid me mine!   820
That malice, not repentance, brought thee hither
By this appears.   I gave, thou say'st, the example
I led the way; bitter reproach, but true;
I to myself was false ere thou to me.
Such pardon, therefore, as I give my folly   825
Take to thy wicked deed; which when thou seest
Impartial, self-severe, inexorable,
Thou wilt renounce thy seeking, and much rather
Confess it feign'd.   Weakness is thy excuse,
And I believe it—weakness to resist   830
Philistian gold: if weakness may excuse,
What murderer, what traitor, parricide,
Incestuous, sacrilegious, but may plead it?
All wickedness is weakness: that plea, therefore,
With God or man will gain thee no remission.   835
But love constrain'd thee!   Call it furious rage
To satisfy thy lust: love seeks to have love;
My love how couldst thou hope, who took'st the way
To raise in me inexpiable hate,
Knowing, as needs I must, by thee betray'd?   840
In vain thou strivest to cover shame with shame,
Or by evasions thy crime uncover'st more.
   Dalila. Since thou determinest weakness for no plea
In man or woman, though to thy own condemning,
Hear what assaults I had, what snares besides,   845
What sieges girt me round, ere I consented;
Which might have awed the best-resolved of men,
The constantest, to have yielded without blame.
It was not gold, as to my charge thou lay'st,
That wrought with me: thou know'st the magistrates   850
And princes of my country came in person,

Solicited, commanded, threaten'd, urged,
Adjured by all the bonds of civil duty
And of religion; press'd how just it was,
How honourable, how glorious, to entrap   855
A common enemy, who had destroy'd
Such numbers of our nation: and the priest
Was not behind, but ever at my ear,
Preaching how meritorious with the gods
It would be to ensnare an irreligious   860
Dishonourer of Dagon.   What had I
To oppose against such powerful arguments?
Only my love of thee held long debate,
And combated in silence all these reasons
With hard contest.   At length, that grounded maxim,   865
So rife and celebrated in the mouths
Of wisest men—that to the public good
Private respects must yield,—with grave authority
Took full possession of me and prevail'd;
Virtue, as I thought, truth, duty, so enjoining.   870
    Samson. I thought where all thy circling wiles would end,
In feign'd religion, smooth hypocrisy!
But had thy love, still odiously pretended,
Been, as it ought, sincere, it would have taught thee
Far other reasonings, brought forth other deeds.   875
I, before all the daughters of my tribe
And of my nation, chose thee from among
My enemies, loved thee, as too well thou knew'st,
Too well; unbosom'd all my secrets to thee,
Not out of levity, but overpower'd   880
By thy request, who could deny thee nothing;
Yet now am judged an enemy.   Why, then,
Didst thou at first receive me for thy husband,
Then, as since then, thy country's foe profess'd?
Being once a wife, for me thou wast to leave   885
Parents and country; nor was I their subject,
Nor under their protection, but my own;
Thou mine, not theirs.   If aught against my life
Thy country sought of thee, it sought unjustly,

Against the law of nature, law of nations; 890
No more thy country, but an impious crew
Of men conspiring to uphold their state
By worse than hostile deeds, violating the ends
For which our country is a name so dear;
Not therefore to be obeyed. But zeal moved thee 895
To please thy gods thou didst it! Gods unable
To acquit themselves and prosecute their foes
But by ungodly deeds, the contradiction
Of their own deity, gods cannot be;
Less therefore to be pleased, obey'd, or fear'd. 900
These false pretexts and varnish'd colours failing
Bare in thy guilt how foul must thou appear!
   Dalila. In argument with men a woman ever
Goes by the worse, whatever be her cause.
   Samson. For want of words, no doubt, or lack of breath!
Witness when I was worried with thy peals. 906
   Dalila. I was a fool, too rash, and quite mistaken
In what I thought would have succeeded best.
Let me obtain forgiveness of thee, Samson;
Afford me place to show what recompense 910
Towards thee I intend for what I have misdone,
Misguided; only what remains past cure
Bear not too sensibly, nor still insist
To afflict thyself in vain; though sight be lost,
Life yet hath many solaces, enjoy'd 915
Where other senses want not their delights,
At home, in leisure and domestic ease,
Exempt from many a care and chance to which
Eyesight exposes daily men abroad.
I to the lords will intercede, not doubting 920
Their favourable ear, that I may fetch thee
From forth this loathsome prison-house, to abide
With me, where my redoubled love and care,
With nursing diligence, to me glad office,
May ever tend about thee to old age, 925
With all things grateful cheer'd, and so supplied
That what by me thou hast lost thou least shall miss.

Samson. No, no; of my condition take no care;
It fits not; thou and I long since are twain;
Nor think me so unwary or accursed   930
To bring my feet again into the snare
Where once I have been caught.   I know thy trains,
Though dearly to my cost, thy gins, and toils;
Thy fair enchanted cup and warbling charms
No more on me have power; their force is null'd;   935
So much of adder's wisdom I have learn'd,
To fence my ear against thy sorceries.
If in my flower of youth and strength, when all men
Loved, honour'd, fear'd me, thou alone could hate me,
Thy husband, slight me, sell me, and forgo me;   940
How wouldst thou use me now, blind, and thereby
Deceivable, in most things as a child
Helpless, thence easily contemn'd, and scorn'd,
And last neglected!   How wouldst thou insult,
When I must live uxorious to thy will,   945
In perfect thraldom! how again betray me,
Bearing my words and doings to the lords
To gloss upon, and, censuring, frown or smile!
This jail I count the house of liberty
To thine, whose doors my feet shall never enter.   950
    Dalila. Let me approach, at least, and touch thy hand.
    Samson. Not for thy life, lest fierce remembrance wake
My sudden rage to tear thee joint by joint.
At distance I forgive thee; go with that;
Bewail thy falsehood, and the pious works   955
It hath brought forth to make thee memorable
Among illustrious women, faithful wives:
Cherish thy hasten'd widowhood with the gold
Of matrimonial treason: so farewell.
    Dalila. I see thou art implacable, more deaf   960
To prayers than winds and seas; yet winds to seas
Are reconciled at length, and sea to shore:
Thy anger, unappeasable, still rages,
Eternal tempest, never to be calm'd.
Why do I humble thus myself, and, suing   965

For peace, reap nothing but repulse and hate,
Bid go with evil omen, and the brand
Of infamy upon my name denounced?
To mix with thy concernments I desist
Henceforth, nor too much disapprove my own.   970
Fame, if not double-faced, is double-mouth'd,
And with contrary blast proclaims most deeds;
On both his wings, one black, the other white,
Bears greatest names in his wild aery flight.
My name, perhaps, among the Circumcised   975
In Dan, in Judah, and the bordering tribes,
To all posterity may stand defamed,
With malediction mention'd, and the blot
Of falsehood most unconjugal traduced.
But in my country, where I most desire,   980
In Ecron, Gaza, Asdod, and in Gath,
I shall be named among the famousest
Of women, sung at solemn festivals,
Living and dead recorded, who, to save
Her country from a fierce destroyer, chose   985
Above the faith of wedlock-bands; my tomb
With odours visited, and annual flowers;
Not less renown'd than in Mount Ephraim
Jael, who with inhospitable guile
Smote Sisera sleeping, through the temples nail'd.   990
Nor shall I count it heinous to enjoy
The public marks of honour and reward
Conferr'd upon me for the piety
Which to my country I was judged to have shown.
At this whoever envies or repines,   995
I leave him to his lot, and like my own.'   [*Exit.*

   Chorus. She's gone,—a manifest serpent by her sting
Discover'd in the end, till now conceal'd.
   Samson. So let her go: God sent her to debase me,
And aggravate my folly, who committed   1000
To such a viper his most sacred trust
Of secrecy, my safety, and my life.
   Chorus. Yet beauty, though injurious, hath strange power,

After offence returning, to regain
Love once possess'd, nor can be easily   1005
Repulsed without much inward passion felt,
And secret sting of amorous remorse.
   Samson. Love-quarrels oft in pleasing concord end,
Not wedlock-treachery endangering life.
   Chorus. It is not virtue, wisdom, valour, wit,   1010
Strength, comeliness of shape, or amplest merit,
That woman's love can win, or long inherit;
But what it is, hard is to say,
Harder to hit,
Which way soever men refer it;   1015
Much like thy riddle, Samson, in one day
Or seven though one should musing sit.
   If any of these, or all, the Timnian bride
Had not so soon preferr'd
Thy paranymph, worthless to thee compared,   1020
Successor in thy bed;
Nor both so loosely disallied
Their nuptials, nor this last so treacherously
Had shorn the fatal harvest of thy head.
Is it for that such outward ornament   1025
Was lavish'd on their sex, that inward gifts
Were left for haste unfinish'd, judgment scant,
Capacity not raised to apprehend
Or value what is best
In choice, but oftest to affect the wrong?   1030
Or was too much of self-love mix'd,
Of constancy no root infix'd.
That either they love nothing, or not long?
   Whate'er it be, to wisest men and best
Seeming at first all heavenly under virgin veil,   1035
Soft, modest, meek, demure,
Once join'd, the contrary she proves, a thorn
Intestine, far within defensive arms
A cleaving mischief, in his way to virtue
Adverse and turbulent; or by her charms   1040
Draws him awry, enslaved

With dotage, and his sense depraved
To folly and shameful deeds which ruin ends.
What pilot so expert but needs must wreck,
Embark'd with such a steers-mate at the helm?   1045
    Favour'd of Heav'n who finds
One virtuous, rarely found,
That in domestic good combines!
Happy that house! his way to peace is smooth:
But virtue which breaks through all opposition,   1050
And all temptation can remove,
Most shines and most is acceptable above.
    Therefore God's universal law
Gave to the man despotic power
Over his female in due awe;   1055
Nor from that right to part an hour,
Smile she or lour:
So shall he least confusion draw
On his whole life, not sway'd
By female usurpation, nor dismay'd.   1060
    But had we best retire? I see a storm.
Samson. Fair days have oft contracted wind and rain.
Chorus. But this another kind of tempest brings.
Samson. Be less abstruse, my riddling days are past.
Chorus. Look now for no enchanting voice, nor fear
The bait of honey'd words; a rougher tongue   1066
Draws hitherward; I know him by his stride,
The giant Harapha of Gath; his look
Haughty as is his pile high-built and proud.
Comes he in peace? What wind hath blown him hither
I less conjecture than when first I saw   1071
The sumptuous Dalila floating this way:
His habit carries peace, his brow defiance.
Samson. Or peace or not, alike to me he comes.
Chorus. His fraught we soon shall know; he now arrives.

HARAPHA.

Harapha. I come not, Samson, to condole thy chance,
As these perhaps, yet wish it had not been,   1077

descended from Giants in bible.

Though for no friendly intent.   I am of Gath;
Men call me Harapha, of stock renown'd
As Og, or Anak, and the Emims old   1080
That Kiriathaim held; thou know'st me now
If thou at all art known.   Much I have heard
Of thy prodigious might and feats perform'd,
Incredible to me, in this displeased,
That I was never present on the place   1085
Of those encounters, where we might have tried
Each other's force in camp or listed field;   — people drawn
And now am come to see of whom such noise   up to fight
Hath walk'd about, and each limb to survey,
If thy appearance answer loud report.   1090
    Samson. The way to know were not to see, but taste.
    Harapha. Dost thou already single me?   I thought = challenge
Gyves and the mill had tamed thee.   O that fortune
Had brought me to the field where thou art famed
To have wrought such wonders with an ass's jaw! 1095
I should have forced thee soon with other arms,
Or left thy carcass where the ass lay thrown:
So had the glory of prowess been recover'd   prowess - valour
To Palestine, won by a Philistine   courage
From the unforeskinn'd race, of whom thou bear'st 1100
The highest name for valiant acts; that honour,
Certain to have won by mortal duel from thee,
I lose, prevented by thy eyes put out.
    Samson. Boast not of what thou wouldst have done, but do
What then thou wouldst; thou seest it in thy hand. 1105
    Harapha. To combat with a blind man I disdain;
And thou hast need much washing to be touch'd.
    Samson. Such usage as your honourable lords
Afford me, assassinated and betray'd;   hyperbole (of Dalila)
Who durst not with their whole united powers   1110
In fight withstand me single and unarm'd,
Nor in the house with chamber-ambushes - people hiding in
Close-banded durst attack me; no, not sleeping,   rooms.
Till they had hired a woman with their gold,
Breaking her marriage-faith, to circumvent me.   1115

outwit

Therefore, without feign'd shifts, let be assign'd
Some narrow place enclosed, where sight may give thee,
Or rather flight, no great advantage on me;
Then put on all thy gorgeous arms, thy helmet
And brigandine of brass, thy broad habergeon,   1120
Vant-brace and greaves and gauntlet; add thy spear,
A weaver's beam, and seven-times-folded shield;
I only with an oaken staff will meet thee,
And raise such outcries on thy clatter'd iron,
Which long shall not withhold me from thy head,   1125
That in a little time, while breath remains thee,
Thou oft shalt wish thyself at Gath, to boast
Again in safety what thou wouldst have done
To Samson, but shalt never see Gath more.

   Harapha. Thou durst not thus disparage glorious arms,
Which greatest heroes have in battle worn,   1131
Their ornament and safety, had not spells,
And black enchantments, some magician's art,
Arm'd thee or charm'd thee strong, which thou from Heaven
Feign'dst at thy birth was given thee in thy hair,   1135
Where strength can least abide, though all thy hairs
Were bristles ranged like those that ridge the back
Of chafed wild boars, or ruffled porcupines.

   Samson. I know no spells, use no forbidden arts;
My trust is in the Living God who gave me   1140
At my nativity this strength, diffused
No less through all my sinews, joints, and bones,
Than thine, while I preserved these locks unshorn,
The pledge of my unviolated vow.
For proof hereof, if Dagon be thy god,   1145
Go to his temple, invoke his aid
With solemnest devotion, spread before him
How highly it concerns his glory now
To frustrate and dissolve these magic spells,
Which I to be the power of Israel's God   1150
Avow, and challenge Dagon to the test;
Offering to combat thee his champion bold,
With the utmost of his godhead seconded;

Then thou shalt see, or rather to thy sorrow
Soon feel, whose God is strongest, thine or mine.   1155
   Harapha. Presume not on thy God, whate'er he be:
Thee he regards not, owns not, hath cut off
Quite from his people, and deliver'd up
Into thine enemies' hand; permitted them
To put out both thine eyes; and fetter'd send thee   1160
Into the common prison, there to grind
Among the slaves and asses thy comrades,
As good for nothing else, no better service,
With those thy boisterous locks—no worthy match
For valour to assail, nor by the sword   1165
Of noble warrior, so to stain his honour,
But by the barber's razor best subdued.
   Samson. All these indignities, for such they are
From thine, these evils I deserve, and more,
Acknowledge them from God inflicted on me   1170
Justly, yet despair not of his final pardon
Whose ear is ever open, and his eye
Gracious to re-admit the suppliant:
In confidence whereof I once again
Defy thee to the trial of mortal fight,   1175
By combat to decide whose god is God,
Thine, or whom I with Israel's sons adore.
   Harapha. Fair honour that thou dost thy God, in trust-
        ing
He will accept thee to defend his cause,
A murderer, a revolter, and a robber!   1180
   Samson. Tongue-doughty giant, how dost thou prove me
these?
   Harapha. Is not thy nation subject to our lords?
Their magistrates confess'd it, when they took thee
As a league-breaker, and deliver'd bound
Into our hands: for hadst thou not committed   1185
Notorious murder on those thirty men
At Ascalon, who never did thee harm;
Then like a robber stripp'dst them of their robes?
The Philistines, when thou hadst broke the league,

Went up with armed powers thee only seeking,   1190
To others did no violence nor spoil.

   Samson. Among the daughters of the Philistines
I chose a wife, which argued me no foe;
And in your city held my nuptial feast:
But your ill-meaning politician lords,   1195
Under pretence of bridal friends and guests,
Appointed to await me thirty spies,
Who, threatening cruel death, constrain'd the bride
To wring from me and tell to them my secret,
That solved the riddle which I had proposed.   1200
When I perceived all set on enmity,
As on my enemies, wherever chanced,
I used hostility and took their spoil
To pay my underminers in their coin.
My nation was subjected to your lords!   1205
It was the force of conquest; force with force
Is well ejected when the conquer'd can.
But I, a private person, whom my country
As a league-breaker gave up bound, presumed
Single rebellion, and did hostile acts!   1210
I was no private, but a person raised
With strength sufficient and command from Heaven
To free my country; if their servile minds
Me, their deliverer sent, would not receive,
But to their masters gave me up for nought,   1215
The unworthier they; whence to this day they serve.
I was to do my part from Heav'n assign'd,
And had perform'd it if my known offence
Had not disabled me, not all your force:
These shifts refuted, answer thy appellant,   1220
Though by his blindness maim'd for high attempts,
Who now defies thee thrice to single fight,
As a petty enterprise of small enforce.

   Harapha. With thee, a man condemn'd, a slave enroll'd,
Due by the law to capital punishment?   1225
To fight with thee no man of arms will deign.

   Samson. Camest thou for this, vain boaster, to survey me,

To descant on my strength, and give thy verdict?
Come nearer; part not hence so slight inform'd;
But take good heed my hand survey not thee.   1230
  Harapha. O Baal-zebub! can my ears unused
Hear these dishonours, and not render death?
  Samson. No man withholds thee; nothing from thy hand
Fear I incurable; bring up thy van;   — vanguard.
My heels are fetter'd, but my fist is free.   1235
  Harapha. This insolence other kind of answer fits.
  Samson. Go, baffled coward, lest I run upon thee,
Though in these chains, bulk without spirit vast;
And with one buffet lay thy structure low,
Or swing thee in the air, then dash thee down   1240
To the hazard of thy brains and shatter'd sides.
  Harapha. By Astaroth, ere long thou shalt lament

Goddess
of moon
+ fertility

These braveries, in irons loaden on thee.   [*Exit.*
  Chorus. His giantship is gone somewhat crest-fallen,
Stalking with less unconscionable strides,   1245
And lower looks, but in a sultry chafe.
  Samson. I dread him not, nor all his giant-brood,
Though fame divulge him father of five sons,
All of gigantic size, Goliah chief.
  Chorus. He will directly to the lords, I fear,   1250
And with malicious counsel stir them up
Some way or other yet further to afflict thee.
  Samson. He must allege some cause, and offer'd fight
Will not dare mention, lest a question rise
Whether he durst accept the offer or not;   1255
And that he durst not plain enough appear'd.
Much more affliction than already felt
They cannot well impose, nor I sustain,
If they intend advantage of my labours,
The work of many hands, which earns my keeping   1260
With no small profit daily to my owners.
But come what will, my deadliest foe will prove
My speediest friend, by death to rid me hence;
The worst that he can give, to me the best.
Yet so it may fall out, because their end   1265

Is hate, not help, to me, it may with mine
Draw their own ruin who attempt the deed.
   Chorus. O how comely it is and how reviving
To the spirits of just men long oppress'd!
When God into the hands of their deliverer   1270
Puts invincible might,
To quell the mighty of the earth, the oppressor,
The brute and boisterous force of violent men,
Hardy and industrious to support
Tyrannic power, but raging to pursue   1275
The righteous and all such as honour truth!
He all their ammunition
And feats of war defeats,
With plain heroic magnitude of mind
And celestial vigour arm'd;   1280
Their armouries and magazines contemns,
Renders them useless, while
With winged expedition
Swift as the lightning glance he executes
His errand on the wicked, who, surprised,   1285
Lose their defence, distracted and amazed.
   But patience is more oft the exercise
Of saints, the trial of their fortitude,
Making them each his own deliverer,
And victor over all   1290
That tyranny or fortune can inflict.
Either of these is in thy lot,
Samson, with might endued
Above the sons of men; but sight bereaved
May chance to number thee with those   1295
Whom patience finally must crown.
   This Idol's day hath been to thee no day of rest,
Labouring thy mind
More than the working day thy hands;
And yet, perhaps, more trouble is behind,   1300
For I descry this way
Some other tending; in his hand
A sceptre or quaint staff he bears,

Comes on amain, speed in his look.
By his habit I discern him now   1305
A public officer, and now at hand:
His message will be short and voluble.

OFFICER.

Officer. Ebrews, the prisoner Samson here I seek.
Chorus. His manacles remark him; there he sits.
Officer. Samson, to thee our lords thus bid me say: 1310
This day to Dagon is a solemn feast,
With sacrifices, triumph, pomp, and games;
Thy strength they know surpassing human rate,
And now some public proof thereof require
To honour this great feast, and great assembly.   1315
Rise therefore with all speed, and come along,
Where I shall see thee hearten'd and fresh clad,
To appear as fits before the illustrious lords.
   Samson. Thou knows't I am an Ebrew; therefore tell them,
Our law forbids at their religious rites   1320
My presence; for that cause I cannot come.
   Officer. This answer, be assured, will not content them.
   Samson. Have they not sword-players, and every sort
Of gymnic artists, wrestlers, riders, runners,
Jugglers and dancers, antics, mummers, mimics,   1325
But they must pick me out, with shackles tired,
And over-labour'd at their public mill,
To make them sport with blind activity?
Do they not seek occasion of new quarrels
On my refusal, to distress me more,   1330
Or make a game of my calamities?
Return the way thou camest; I will not come.
   Officer. Regard thyself; this will offend them highly.
   Samson. Myself! my conscience, and internal peace.
Can they think me so broken, so debased   1335
With corporal servitude, that my mind ever
Will condescend to such absurd commands?
Although their drudge, to be their fool or jester,
And in my midst of sorrow and heart-grief

To show them feats, and play before their god—   1340
The worst of all indignities, yet on me
Join'd with extreme contempt! I will not come.

  Officer. My message was imposed on me with speed,
Brooks no delay: is this thy resolution?   1344

  Samson. So take it with what speed thy message needs.

  Officer. I am sorry what this stoutness will produce. [*Exit.*

  Samson. Perhaps thou shalt have cause to sorrow indeed.

  Chorus. Consider, Samson; matters now are strain'd
Up to the highth, whether to hold or break:
He's gone; and who knows how he may report   1350
Thy words by adding fuel to the flame?
Expect another message, more imperious,
More lordly thundering than thou well wilt bear.

  Samson. Shall I abuse this consecrated gift
Of strength, again returning with my hair,   1355
After my great transgression? so requite
Favour renew'd, and add a greater sin
By prostituting holy things to idols,
A Nazarite in place abominable
Vaunting my strength in honour to their Dagon?   1360
Besides how vile, contemptible, ridiculous,
What act more execrably unclean, profane?

  Chorus. Yet with this strength thou servest the Philistines,
Idolatrous, uncircumcised, unclean.

  Samson. Not in their idol-worship, but by labour   1365
Honest and lawful, to deserve my food
Of those who have me in their civil power.

  Chorus. Where the heart joins not, outward acts defile not.

  Samson. Where outward force constrains, the sentence
    holds:
But who constrains me to the temple of Dagon,   1370
Not dragging? The Philistian lords command:
Commands are no constraints. If I obey them,
I do it freely, venturing to displease
God for the fear of man, and man prefer,
Set God behind: which in his jealousy   1375
Shall never, unrepented, find forgiveness.

Yet that he may dispense with me, or thee,
Present in temples at idolatrous rites
For some important cause, thou need'st not doubt.
    Chorus. How thou wilt here come off surmounts my reach.
    Samson. Be of good courage; I begin to feel   1381
Some rousing motions in me, which dispose
To something extraordinary my thoughts.
I with this messenger will go along,
Nothing to do, be sure, that may dishonour   1385
Our law, or stain my vow of Nazarite.
If there be aught of presage in the mind,
This day will be remarkable in my life
By some great act, or of my days the last.
    Chorus. In time thou hast resolved; the man returns. 1390
    Officer. Samson, this second message from our lords
To thee I am bid say: Art thou our slave,
Our captive, at the public mill our drudge,
And darest thou at our sending and command
Dispute thy coming? Come without delay;   1395
Or we shall find such engines to assail
And hamper thee, as thou shalt come of force,
Though thou wert firmlier fasten'd than a rock.
    Samson. I could be well content to try their art,
Which to no few of them would prove pernicious;   1400
Yet, knowing their advantages too many,
Because they shall not trail me through their streets
Like a wild beast, I am content to go.
Masters' commands come with a power resistless
To such as owe them absolute subjection;   1405
And for a life who will not change his purpose?
(So mutable are all the ways of men!)
Yet this be sure, in nothing to comply
Scandalous or forbidden in our law.
    Officer. I praise thy resolution. Doff these links: 1410
By this compliance thou wilt win the lords
To favour, and perhaps to set thee free.
    Samson. Brethren, farewell: your company along
I will not wish, lest it perhaps offend them

To see me girt with friends; and how the sight   1415
Of me, as of a common enemy,
So dreaded once, may now exasperate them
I know not.   Lords are lordliest in their wine;
And the well-feasted priest then soonest fired
With zeal, if aught religion seem concern'd;   1420
No less the people, on their holy-days,
Impetuous, insolent, unquenchable:
Happen what may, of me expect to hear
Nothing dishonourable, impure, unworthy
Our God, our law, my nation, or myself;   1425
The last of me or no I cannot warrant.

                [*Exeunt* SAMSON *and the* OFFICER.

   Chorus. Go, and the Holy One
Of Israel be thy guide
To what may serve his glory best, and spread his name
Great among the heathen round;   1430
Send thee the Angel of thy birth, to stand
Fast by thy side, who from thy father's field
Rode up in flames after his message told
Of thy conception, and be now a shield
Of fire; that Spirit that first rush'd on thee   1435
In the camp of Dan
Be efficacious in thee now at need!
For never was from Heaven imparted
Measure of strength so great to mortal seed,
As in thy wondrous actions hath been seen.   1440
But wherefore comes old Manoa in such haste
With youthful steps?   Much livelier than erewhile
He seems: supposing here to find his son,
Or of him bringing to us some glad news?

MANOA.

   Manoa. Peace with you, brethren! My inducement hither
Was not at present here to find my son,   1446
By order of the lords new parted hence
To come and play before them at their feast.
I heard all as I came, the city rings,

And numbers thither flock; I had no will,   1450
Lest I should see him forced to things unseemly.
But that which moved my coming now was chiefly
To give ye part with me what hope I have
With good success to work his liberty.
   Chorus. That hope would much rejoice us to partake
With thee: say, reverend sire; we thirst to hear.   1456
   Manoa. I have attempted, one by one, the lords
Either at home, or through the high street passing,
With supplication prone and father's tears,
To accept of ransom for my son their prisoner.   1460
Some much averse I found, and wondrous harsh,
Contemptuous, proud, set on revenge and spite;
That part most reverenced Dagon and his priests:
Others more moderate seeming, but their aim
Private reward, for which both God and State   1465
They easily would set to sale: a third
More generous far and civil, who confess'd
They had enough revenged, having reduced
Their foe to misery beneath their fears:
The rest was magnanimity to remit,   1470
If some convenient ransom were proposed—
What noise or shout was that? It tore the sky.
   Chorus. Doubtless the people shouting to behold
Their once great dread, captive and blind before them,
Or at some proof of strength before them shown.   1475
   Manoa. His ransom, if my whole inheritance
May compass it, shall willingly be paid
And number'd down: much rather I shall choose
To live the poorest in my tribe, than richest,
And he in that calamitous prison left.   1480
No, I am fix'd not to part hence without him.
For his redemption, all my patrimony,
If need be, I am ready to forgo
And quit: not wanting him, I shall want nothing.
   Chorus. Fathers are wont to lay up for their sons,   1485
Thou for thy son art bent to lay out all;
Sons wont to nurse their parents in old age,

Thou in old age carest how to nurse thy son,
Made older than thy age through eye-sight lost.

   Manoa. It shall be my delight to tend his eyes,   1490
And view him sitting in his house, ennobled
With all those high exploits by him achieved,
And on his shoulders waving down those locks,
That of a nation arm'd the strength contain'd.
And I persuade me, God had not permitted   1495
His strength again to grow up with his hair,
Garrison'd round about him like a camp
Of faithful soldiery, were not his purpose
To use him further yet in some great service—
Not to sit idle with so great a gift   1500
Useless, and thence ridiculous, about him.
And, since his strength with eye-sight was not lost,
God will restore him eye-sight to his strength.

   Chorus. Thy hopes are not ill founded, nor seem vain,
Of his delivery, and thy joy thereon   1505
Conceived agreeable to a father's love,
In both which we, as next, participate.

   Manoa. I know your friendly minds and—Oh! what noise!
Mercy of Heaven! What hideous noise was that?
Horribly loud, unlike the former shout.   1510

   Chorus. Noise call you it, or universal groan
As if the whole inhabitation perish'd?
Blood, death, and deathful deeds are in that noise;
Ruin, destruction at the utmost point.

   Manoa. Of ruin indeed methought I heard the noise:
Oh! it continues; they have slain my son.   1516

   Chorus. Thy son is rather slaying them; that outcry
From slaughter of one foe could not ascend.

   Manoa. Some dismal accident it needs must be;
What shall we do, stay here, or run and see?   1520

   Chorus. Best keep together here, lest, running thither,
We unawares run into danger's mouth.
This evil on the Philistines is fall'n:
From whom could else a general cry be heard?
The sufferers then will scarce molest us here;   1525

From other hands we need not much to fear.
What if, his eye-sight (for to Israel's God
Nothing is hard) by miracle restored,
He now be dealing dole among his foes,
And over heaps of slaughter'd walk his way?   1530
   Manoa. That were a joy presumptuous to be thought.
   Chorus. Yet God hath wrought things as incredible
For his people of old; what hinders now?
   Manoa. He can, I know, but doubt to think he will;
Yet hope would fain subscribe, and tempts belief.   1535
A little stay will bring some notice hither.
   Chorus. Of good or bad so great, of bad the sooner;
For evil news rides post, while good news baits.
And to our wish I see one hither speeding,—
An Ebrew, as I guess, and of our tribe.   1540
   Messenger. O whither shall I run, or which way fly
The sight of this so horrid spectacle,
Which erst my eyes beheld, and yet behold?
For dire imagination still pursues me.
But providence or instinct of nature seems,   1545
Or reason, though disturb'd and scarce consulted,
To have guided me aright, I know not how,
To thee first, reverend Manoa, and to these
My countrymen, whom here I knew remaining,
As at some distance from the place of horror,   1550
So in the sad event too much concern'd.
   Manoa. The accident was loud, and here before thee
With rueful cry; yet what it was we hear not:
No preface needs; thou seest we long to know.
   Messenger. It would burst forth; but I recover breath,
And sense distract, to know well what I utter.   1556
   Manoa. Tell us the sum, the circumstance defer.
   Messenger. Gaza yet stands; but all her sons are fallen;
All in a moment overwhelm'd and fall'n.
   Manoa. Sad! but thou know'st to Israelites not saddest,
The desolation of a hostile city.   1561
   Messenger. Feed on that first; there may in grief be sur-
     feit.

Manoa. Relate by whom.

Messenger.   By Samson.

Manoa.   That still lessens
The sorrow, and converts it nigh to joy.

Messenger. Ah! Manoa, I refrain too suddenly   1565
To utter what will come at last too soon;
Lest evil tidings, with too rude irruption
Hitting thy aged ear, should pierce too deep.

Manoa. Suspense in news is torture; speak them out.

Messenger. Take then the worst in brief: Samson is dead.

Manoa. The worst indeed! O all my hope's defeated
To free him hence! but Death who sets all free
Hath paid his ransom now and full discharge.
What windy joy this day had I conceived,
Hopeful of his delivery, which now proves   1575
Abortive as the first-born bloom of spring
Nipp'd with the lagging rear of winter's frost!
Yet, ere I give the reins to grief, say first,
How died he? death to life is crown or shame.
All by him fell, thou say'st: by whom fell he?   1580
What glorious hand gave Samson his death's wound?

Messenger. Unwounded of his enemies he fell.

Manoa. Wearied with slaughter then, or how? explain.

Messenger. By his own hands.

Manoa.   Self-violence? What cause
Brought him so soon at variance with himself,   1585
Among his foes?

Messenger.   Inevitable cause,
At once both to destroy and be destroy'd:
The edifice, where all were met to see him,
Upon their heads and on his own he pull'd.

Manoa. O lastly over-strong against thyself!   1590
A dreadful way thou took'st to thy revenge.
More than enough we know; but, while things yet
Are in confusion, give us, if thou canst,
Eye-witness of what first or last was done,
Relation more particular and distinct.   1595

Messenger. Occasions drew me early to this city;

business.

And as the gates I enter'd with sun-rise,
The morning trumpets festival proclaim'd
Through each high street.   Little I had dispatch'd,
When all abroad was rumour'd that this day   1600
Samson should be brought forth, to show the people
Proof of his mighty strength in feats and games.
I sorrow'd at his captive state, but minded
Not to be absent at that spectacle.
The building was a spacious theatre,   1605
Half round on two main pillars vaulted high,
With seats where all the lords, and each degree
Of sort, might sit in order to behold;
The other side was open, where the throng
On banks and scaffolds under sky might stand: 1610
I among these aloof obscurely stood.
The feast and noon grew high, and sacrifice
Had fill'd their hearts with mirth, high cheer, and wine,
When to their sports they turn'd.   Immediately
Was Samson as a public servant brought,   1615
In their state livery clad; before him pipes
And timbrels; on each side went armed guards,
Both horse and foot before him and behind,
Archers and slingers, cataphracts and spears.
At sight of him the people with a shout   1620
Rifted the air, clamouring their god with praise,
Who had made their dreadful enemy their thrall.
He, patient but undaunted, where they led him,
Came to the place; and what was set before him,
Which without help of eye might be assay'd,   1625
To heave, pull, draw, or break, he still perform'd
All with incredible, stupendious force,
None daring to appear antagonist.
At length, for intermission sake, they led him
Between the pillars; he his guide requested   1630
(For so from such as nearer stood we heard),
As over-tired, to let him lean a while
With both his arms on those two massy pillars
That to the arched roof gave main support.

He unsuspicious led him; which when Samson   1635
Felt in his arms, with head a while inclined,
And eyes fast fix'd, he stood, as one who pray'd,
Or some great matter in his mind revolved.
At last, with head erect, thus cried aloud:—
"Hitherto, lords, what your commands imposed   1640
I have perform'd, as reason was, obeying,
Not without wonder or delight beheld.
Now, of my own accord, such other trial
I mean to show you of my strength, yet greater,
As with amaze shall strike all who behold."   1645
This utter'd, straining all his nerves he bow'd;
As with the force of winds and waters pent
When mountains tremble, those two massy pillars
With horrible convulsion to and fro
He tugg'd, he shook, till down they came, and drew   1650
The whole roof after them with burst of thunder
Upon the heads of all who sat beneath,
Lords, ladies, captains, counsellors, or priests,
Their choice nobility and flower, not only
Of this, but each Philistian city round,   1655
Met from all parts to solemnize this feast.
Samson, with these immix'd, inevitably
Pull'd down the same destruction on himself;
The vulgar only scaped who stood without.

   Chorus. O dearly bought revenge, yet glorious!   1660
Living or dying thou hast fulfill'd
The work for which thou wast foretold
To Israel, and now liest victorious
Among thy slain self-kill'd;
Not willingly, but tangled in the fold   1665
Of dire Necessity, whose law in death conjoin'd
Thee with thy slaughter'd foes, in number more
Than all thy life had slain before.

   1 *Semichorus.* While their hearts were jocund and sublime,
Drunk with idolatry, drunk with wine,   1670
And fat regorged of bulls and goats,
Chanting their idol, and preferring

Before our living Dread who dwells
In Silo his bright sanctuary:
Among them he a spirit of frenzy sent,   1675
Who hurt their minds,
And urged them on with mad desire
To call in haste for their destroyer:
They only set on sport and play
Unweetingly importuned   1680
Their own destruction to come speedy upon them.
So fond are mortal men
Fall'n into wrath divine,
As their own ruin on themselves to invite,
Insensate left, or to sense reprobate,   1685
And with blindness internal struck.
   2 *Semichorus.* But he, though blind of sight,
Despised, and thought extinguish'd quite,
With inward eyes illuminated,
His fiery virtue roused   1690
From under ashes into sudden flame,
And as an evening dragon came, *as Samson*
Assailant on the perched roosts, *& Philras*
And nests in order ranged *catastrophic.*
Of tame villatic fowl; but as an eagle   1695
His cloudless thunder bolted on their heads.
So Virtue, given for lost,
Depress'd and overthrown, as seem'd,
Like that self-begotten bird
In the Arabian woods emboss'd, *shut in.*   1700
That no second knows nor third,
And lay erewhile in a holocaust,
From out her ashy womb now teem'd,
Revives, reflourishes, then vigorous most
When most unactive deem'd;   1705
And, though her body die, her fame survives,
centuries old A secular bird, ages of lives.
   Manoa. Come, come; no time for lamentation now,
Nor much more cause: Samson hath quit himself
Like Samson, and heroically hath finished   1710

N.B. Continual use of words in radical sense

A life heroic, on his enemies
Fully revenged; hath left them years of mourning,
And lamentation to the sons of Caphtor
Through all Philistian bounds; to Israel
Honour hath left and freedom, let but them   1715
Find courage to lay hold on this occasion;
To himself and father's house eternal fame;
And, which is best and happiest yet, all this
With God not parted from him, as was fear'd,
But favouring and assisting to the end.   1720
Nothing is here for tears, nothing to wail
Or knock the breast; no weakness, no contempt,
Dispraise, or blame; nothing but well and fair,
And what may quiet us in a death so noble.
Let us go find the body where it lies   1725
Soak'd in his enemies' blood, and from the stream
With lavers pure and cleansing herbs wash off
The clotted gore.   I, with what speed the while
(Gaza is not in plight to say us nay),
Will send for all my kindred, all my friends,   1730
To fetch him hence, and solemnly attend
With silent obsequy and funeral train
Home to his father's house.   There will I build him
A monument, and plant it round with shade
Of laurel ever green, and branching palm,   1735
With all his trophies hung, and acts enroll'd
In copious legend, or sweet lyric song.
Thither shall all the valiant youth resort,
And from his memory inflame their breasts
To matchless valour and adventures high: 1740
The virgins also shall, on feastful days,
Visit his tomb with flowers, only bewailing
His lot unfortunate in nuptial choice,
From whence captivity and loss of eyes.
    Chorus. All is best, though we oft doubt,   1745
What the unsearchable dispose
Of Highest Wisdom brings about,
And ever best found in the close.

Oft he seems to hide his face,
But unexpectedly returns;   1750
And to his faithful champion hath in place
Bore witness gloriously; whence Gaza mourns,
And all that band them to resist
His uncontrollable intent;
His servants he, with new acquist   1755
Of true experience from this great event,
With peace and consolation hath dismiss'd,
And calm of mind, all passion spent.

NOTES

THE PREFACE.

1. **as it was anciently composed,** *i.e.* the classical Greek tragedy as opposed to the romantic English tragedy of the sixteenth and seventeenth centuries.

2, 3. **the gravest...of all other poems,** *i.e.* 'graver than all other poems'. For the construction, a Latinism, compare *Paradise Lost*, iv. 323:

> "Adam, the goodliest man of men since born
> His sons; the fairest of her daughters Eve".

3. **said by Aristotle.** The reference is to the passage in Aristotle's *Poetics*, quoted on the title-page of the play. The full quotation is: Τραγῳδία μίμησις πράξεως σπουδαίας . . . δι' ἐλέου καὶ φόβου περαίνουσα τὴν τῶν τοιούτων παθημάτων κάθαρσιν. Aristotle, Poet. vi. Tragoedia est imitatio actionis seriae . . . per misericordiam et metum perficiens talium affectuum lustrationem. For the various interpretations which scholars have given of Aristotle's meaning, see the chapter on 'The Function of Tragedy', in Prof. S. H. Butcher's *Aristotle's Theory of Poetry and Fine Art*. Milton's own interpretation may be illustrated by the closing words of the Chorus in lines 1755-8:

> "His servants he, with new acquist
> Of true experience from this great event,
> With peace and consolation hath dismiss'd,
> And calm of mind, all passion spent".

9. **in physic,** the doctrine *similia similibus curantur* is the foundation of what is known as 'homeopathy'.

15. The verse φθείρουσιν ἤθη χρήσθ' ὁμιλίαι κακαί ('Evil communications corrupt good manners') is found both amongst the fragments of Euripides and those of Menander.

16. **Paraeus.** The Graecised form of the name of the Calvinist theologian Wängler, a Silesian, who lived 1548-1622, and wrote amongst other things a commentary on the *Revelations*, which was translated into English in 1644.

77

21. Dionysius the elder, tyrant of Syracuse from 405-367. In 367 he won the first prize at the Athenian dramatic festival of Lenaea with a tragedy, and is said to have died of joy.

22. Augustus Caesar, said by Suetonius to have written a tragedy on Ajax, and to have thought it so bad that he destroyed it.

24. Lucius Annaeus **Seneca,** the philosopher, was tutor to Nero, and died A.D. 65. It is very doubtful whether he wrote the stilted tragedies which go under his name, and which had so profound an influence on the Italian and English drama of the Renascence. The names of the plays are the *Troas, Thyestes, Hercules Furens, Hercules Oetaeus, Oedipus, Octavia, Medea, Agamemnon, Hippolytus, Thebais.* Cf. J. W. Cunliffe, *The Influence of Seneca on Elizabethan Tragedy.*

26, 27. Gregory Nazianzen was Bishop of Constantinople, and lived circ. 325-390. The play of *Christus Patiens,* formerly inscribed to him, has been shown to be really by some writer of about the twelfth century.

31, 32. other common interludes, the public stage-plays of Milton's own day, with their romantic mixture of tragic and comic interest. They were called 'interludes' because they began as *ludi,* entertainments, *inter,* between the courses of a banquet.

37. no Prologue, no address to the audience, such as we find prefixed to most of Ben Jonson's plays and a few of Shakespeare's, e.g. *Henry V.* For the original sense of πρόλογος in Greek drama, see note on lines 1-114.

38. Martial. The first book of Martial's *Epigrams* begins with a prose *Epistola ad Lectorem.*

46-53. The choruses of Aeschylus and Sophocles are always divided into pairs of stanzas, known as Strophes and Antistrophes, which correspond metrically and in the dance-steps which accompanied them. These were closed by a single stanza or Epode. Euripides, however, introduced a more irregular form of lyric, which is probably what Milton here means by Apolelymenon (Gk. ἀπολελύμενος, loosed), as being freed from the laws of antistrophic correspondence, and Allaeostropha (Gk. ἀλλοῖος, other in kind, στροφή, stanza), or divided into stanzas which do not correspond.

57. the fifth act, the five acts of a Greek play are exclusive of the Prologue and Exodos.

58. intricate or explicit, the 'complicated' (πεπλεγμένος) or 'straightforward' (ἁπλῆ) of Aristotle, *Poetics,* ch. x.

67. twenty-four hours. This is the law of Unity of Time as laid down by Aristotle (*Poetics,* v. 4).

The Prologue.—Lines 1-114.

Samson enters (1-11) leaning upon the arm of a guide, who is not mentioned in the list of *dramatis personæ,* and who takes no part in the dialogue, being what the Greeks call a κωφόν πρόσωπον or mute character. Samson explains his absence from toil on the Philistian holiday (11-22), and briefly refers to the chief incidents of his life, to his sin and his punishment (23-79). He then breaks into a lyrical dirge over his loss of sight (80-109). Such lyrical passages, put in the mouth not of the chorus but of an actor, were called in Greek tragedy τὰ ἀπὸ τῆς σκηνῆς, songs from the stage, the position of the chorus being not with the actors upon the stage but beneath it in the orchestra. If the lyric passage was, as here, a soliloquy, it was called a μονῳδία, a song of one man. Finally, Samson breaks off on hearing the approach of the chorus (110-114).

Milton follows the practice of the Attic tragedians in using the Prologue or πρόλογος to recapitulate the previous history of the hero, and of Aeschylus in particular in throwing it into the form of a soliloquy. The narrative is not really complete without a previous knowledge of the story, but on this Milton, like his classical masters, was entitled to count.

1. Cf. the opening of Sophocles' *Oedipus Coloneus*, where Antigone leads her father on to the stage, and the passage of Euripides' *Phoenissae*, where the blind Teiresias is similarly led on by his daughter.

thy, spoken to the guide.

2. dark, in the sense of 'blind', transferred from the eyes to the feet. Milton seems to be translating from the passage of the *Phoenissae* already referred to, l. 834:

ὡς τυφλῷ ποδὶ
ὀφθαλμὸς εἶ σύ,

('Since to the blind foot thou art an eye').

4. There I am wont to sit. Richardson, the painter, described Milton as wont to sit, towards the end of his life, "at the door of his house, near Bunhill Fields, without Moorgate, in warm sunny weather, to enjoy the fresh air".

11. day-spring, a Biblical word for 'dawn'. Cf. *S. Luke*, i. 78, "the day-spring from on high hath visited us".

12. solemn. Verity suggests the sense of the Latin *solemnis*, recurring annually; but the more ordinary English sense suits just as well here.

13. Dagon, their sea-idol, the god of Philistia, half-man, half-fish, perhaps identical with a deity of Babylonia, called upon inscriptions Dakan or Dagon. He is described among the infernal host in *Paradise Lost*, i. 462-466:

"Dagon his name, sea-monster, upward man
And downward fish; yet had his temple high
Rear'd in Azotus, dreaded through the coast
Of Palestine, in Gath and Ascalon
And Accaron and Gaza's frontier bounds".

Cf. also the account of the fall of Dagon in *1 Sam.*, v. 1-5.

18. Such a line as this, repeating and lingering over one word from a previous line, is very characteristic of Milton. Cf. lines 270, 271.

19. Cf. l. 623: "Thoughts my tormentors, arm'd with deadly stings".

20. no sooner found alone, as soon as I am found alone. The use of a participial clause for an adverbial clause of time is one of Milton's Latinisms; but in Latin the case of the participle would prevent any ambiguity, whereas here there is a momentary doubt whether 'found' goes with 'hornets' or 'me'.

23, 24. foretold Twice by an Angel. Cf. *Judges*, xiii. 3–5 and 9–21.

27. charioting, removing as in a chariot.

31. separate. The adjective is used in the original participial sense of the Latin *separatus*, set apart. This is the proper sense of the Hebrew word rendered *Nazarite*. Cf. *Numbers*, vi. 2, "When either man or woman shall separate themselves to vow a vow of a Nazarite, to separate themselves unto the Lord".

33. captived. Here we may, as in l. 694 we must, use the Latin accent *captiv'ed*; but we may also treat the foot as trochaic, and accent *cap'tived*. Cf. Essay on Metre, §§ 10, 12 (ii).

34. gaze, object to gaze at. Cf. l. 567: "to visitants a gaze".

38. Promise was. Cf. *Judges*, xiii. 5.

46. This is the key-note of the tragedy. Samson did not only fail; he failed through his own fault; and though after repentance he has a new opportunity, yet it carries with it his own destruction.

47–49. The construction is somewhat loose; but the sense is 'could not keep secret in what part this high gift was lodged, and how easily it might be bereft me'.

50. a woman, *i.e.* Dalila. Cf. ll. 235, 236, 732–1009, and *Judges*, xvi. 16, 17.

53. Cf. Horace, *Odes*, iii. 4. 65: *Vis consili expers mole ruit sua.*

55. secure; in the common sense of the Latin *securus*, falsely confident.

63. Suffices, it suffices: the pronoun is dropped in imitation of the Latin *sufficit*.

65. each seems to be used both as the subject of 'ask' and the object of 'wait'.

66. With Samson's lamentation over his loss of sight, which of course recalls Milton's own blindness, cf. *Paradise Lost*, iii. 21–50.

68. Blind among enemies, *i.e.* 'to be blind among enemies'.

70. prime, in the radical sense of the Latin *primus*, first in order of time: cf. the account of the first day of creation in *Genesis*, i. 3: "And God said, Let there be light: and there was light".

73. **Inferior** is loosely connected with the idea of 'me' taken out of the 'my' of the preceding line.

74. **here,** in this point of sight.

75. **dark in light.** Milton is fond of such juxtapositions of contrasted ideas. The figure is known by grammarians as Oxymoron. Cf. l. 100, 'a living death', and *Paradise Lost*, ii. 142, 143:

> "Thus repulsed, our final hope
> Is flat despair";

and iii. 380:

> "Dark with excessive bright thy skirts appear";

and x. 788:

> "I shall die a living death".

76. **daily fraud.** One recalls the story that Milton's daughters sold his books to a rag shop during his blindness.

80. With the beginning of the lyric passage, Samson's lament has a more impassioned tone.

81. Mr. Bridges (p. 36) would scan this line with three trochaic feet, thus:

> Írre- | cóvẹra- | bly dárk, | tótal | eclípse.

I prefer to make the first foot an anapaest and not to elide the e, thus:

> Irrecó- | vera- | bly dárk, | tótal | eclípse.

Cf. Essay on Metre, § 16 (ii).

83. **thou great Word.** Cf. l. 70, note.

85. **prime,** first, as in l. 70.

87. **silent.** Of course the sun always is silent; but Milton has in mind the Latin term *luna silens*, used of the moon when she does not shine, between the waning of the old and the rising of the new moon. This period was called the *interlunium*. Cf. Pliny, *Natural History*, i. 16, 39: *Quem diem alii interlunii, alii silentis lunae appellant.* Mr. Churton Collins quotes Dante, *Inferno*, i. 60: "*Mi ripingeva la dove il sol tace*" ('I hid myself there where the sun is silent').

89. **her vacant interlunar cave;** the cave where the moon may be supposed to spend her *interlunium*. But why *vacant*? It is rather the sky than the cave that is vacant at that period. Perhaps 'the cave where the moon is vacant', in the sense of the Latin *vacat opera*, rests, takes vacation from business.

93. **She,** *i.e.* the soul; Milton might have found this notion of the soul diffused through thè body in Augustine *De Origine Animae* —*per omnes eius [corporis] particulas tota simul adest…in omnibus tota et in singulis tota.*

95. **obvious;** in the radical Latin sense of 'placed in the way', from *ob viam.*

95. quench'd, robbed of light. Cf. *Paradise Lost*, iii. **25, 26**:

"So thick a drop serene hath quenched their orbs,
Or dim suffusion veiled".

98. exiled. Both Shakespeare and Milton generally scan, as here, *exíled*.

100. a living death: cf. l. 75 note, and the passage from *Paradise Lost*, x. 788, there quoted.

102. Myself my sepulchre: cf. l. 156, "The dungeon of thyself".

106. obnoxious, in the common sense of the Latin *obnoxius*, exposed to.

110. with joint pace goes with 'steering', not with 'I hear'. The sense is 'moving in time', as the chorus of course did.

111. steering this way. Cf. *Ode on the Nativity*, 144–146:

"Mercy will sit between,
Throned in celestial sheen,
With radiant feet the tissued clouds down steering".

114. The whole line is in apposition to 'to insult'.

The Parodos.—Lines 115–175.

The πάροδος or entry-song was the march sung by the Greek tragic Chorus, as it filed for the first time into the orchestra; or, if the Chorus was 'on' from the beginning, the first choric ode. In Milton, as in the earlier Greek tragedians, the choruses are not, as in Euripides, mere interludes only slightly connected with the plot; they are used to enforce the ethical or emotional aspects of the action. Here the Chorus lays stress on the former splendour, the fall and the misery of Samson.

118. diffused, in the radical sense of the Latin *diffundere*, 'to pour out': properly used of inanimate things, and here of the semi-animate limbs of the worn-out Samson. There may be a reminiscence in the 'diffused' and 'languish'd' of this line and the next of Ovid, *Ex Ponto*, iii. 3, 8: *fusaque erant toto languida membra toro*.

122. weeds, raiment. Cf. Glossary.

128. Cf. *Judges*, xiv. 6.

129. embattled, ranked in order of battle.

131. forgery; in the radical sense of the 'forging' of metal.

133. Chalybean-temper'd steel. The joint-epithet = 'tempered by the Chalybes'. Cf. Glossary, s.v. *temper*. *Chalybéan* is the usual accent; here it is *Chaly'bean*. The Chalybes were a people in the north of Asia Minor, famous as metal workers.

134. Adamantean proof, 'as invincible as adamant'. Cf. Glossary, s.vv. *adamantean, proof*. 'Proof' is here a noun, and the

noun and its adjective are used together as an adjective to 'mail'.
This is a peculiarity of Milton's. Cf. Essay on Milton's English, § 5 (e).

136. insupportably, unendurably.

advanced. A reminiscence of Shakespeare, *Coriolanus*, ii.
1. 177:

"Death, that dark spirit, in's nervy arm doth lie;
 Which, being advanced, declines, and then men die".

138. Ascalonite. Ascalon was a city of Philistia. Cf. *Judges*,
xiv. 19.

139. his lion ramp, Samson's lion-like spring. We still speak
heraldically of 'a lion rampant'. Cf. Glossary, s.v. *ramp*.

142–145. Cf. *Judges*, xv. 9–17.

144. foreskins, uncircumcised men, a contemptuous term used
by the circumcised Jews for their Philistine neighbours. The foreskin
is the part of the body cut off in the rite of circumcision.

145. Ramath-lechi. The Hebrew name of the place is inter-
preted in the glossary of the Authorized Version as 'the lifting up of
the jawbone' or 'the casting away of the jawbone'. But *Ramath*
= 'eminence', 'hill', rather than 'lifting up'. Probably the place
was so called from its resemblance in shape to a jaw-bone, and the
legend invented to justify the name.

146–150. Cf. *Judges*, xvi. 1–3.

146. Note the omission of the subject, on which see Essay on
Milton's English, § 5 (a).

147. Azza, a variant of the name Gaza.

148. Hebron, seat of giants. Hebron was a city in Judah.
Cf. *Joshua*, xv. 13, 14: "Unto Caleb...he gave...Hebron. And
Caleb drove thence the three sons of Anak, Sheshai, and Ahiman,
and Talmai, the children of Anak"; and *Numbers*, xiii. 33: "And
there we saw the giants, the sons of Anak, which come of the
giants: and we were in our own sight as grasshoppers, and so we
were in their sight".

149. No journey of a Sabbath-day. The Jews were limited
to three-quarters of a mile on the Sabbath. Hebron and Gaza are
forty miles apart.

150. The reference is to the Titan Atlas, who bore up the heavens
in Greek myth.

Like whom. On the omission of the antecedent, cf. Essay on
Milton's English, § 5 (d).

154. Inseparably dark, dark with a darkness that cannot be put
away.

156. Cf. l. 102.

157. The allusion is to the notion of Platonic philosophy, that the
soul is confined, fettered, or imprisoned in the body.

159. real, physical, as opposed to the metaphorical darkness of the soul in the body.

161. incorporate, become one with; we should use the passive, 'be incorporated with'.

163. visual beam, ray of light, the notion being that the ray was rather projected from, than directed to the eye.

164. mirror, that in which we see the image of the variable fortune of all men reflected.

165. Since man on earth, since man was born on earth. On the Latinism, cf. Essay on Milton's English, § 6 (c).

172. the sphere of fortune. Fortune is represented, sometimes, as standing on a sphere or globe; sometimes as turning a wheel on which mortals revolve. Cf. e.g. Burne-Jones' well-known picture and Tennyson's lines:

> "Turn, Fortune, turn thy wheel with smile or frown;
> With that wild wheel we go not up or down".

The First Episode.—Lines 176–292.

The Chorus attempts to console Samson. In the dialogue that follows, Samson lays stress on his own fault as the occasion of his failure and suffering. He also blames the ingratitude of the Israelites towards him. Of his own offending the head and front is the sensual sin of meddling with the Philistine women.

The ἐπεισόδιον or 'episode' of a Greek play is the name given to the intervals of dialogue between two choric songs. Literally it means 'that which follows on the εἴσοδος or entrance of the chorus'. Roughly it corresponds to the modern 'scene', although the action of a Greek play was only broken by the choruses.

Lines 277–289 do not form a regular choric ode. It was not unusual for the chorus in the early Greek drama to intervene in the dialogue with a short lyrical passage.

177. unjointed, disconnected.

181. Eshtaol and Zora, towns of Dan. Cf. *Judges*, xiii. 2; xvi. 31.

184. Cf. Aeschylus, *Prometheus Vinctus*, 378:

> ὀργῆς νοσούσης εἰσὶν ἰατροὶ λόγοι

('Words are the physicians of diseased passion').

189. friends, *i.e.* the word 'friends'.

190. superscription, used for the 'inscription' on a coin in *S. Matthew*, xxii. 20: "Whose is this image and superscription?"

of the most, as referring to the majority.

191. Cf. Ovid *Tristia*, i. 9. 5–6:

> "*Donec eris felix, multos numerabis amicos;*
> *Tempora si fuerint nubila, solus eris*".

197. heave, raise. Cf. *L'Allegro*, 145-147:

> "That Orpheus' self may heave his head
> From golden slumber on a bed
> Of heaped Elysian flowers".

203. proverb'd, made a proverb of. Cf. Essay on Milton's English, § 6 (*c*). Shakespeare uses the noun in a very similar sense in *Romeo and Juliet*, i. 4. 37: "I am proverbed with a grandsire phrase", *i.e.* 'the old proverb of our grandsires applies to me'.

207. mean, moderate, average.

208, 209. 'My wisdom ought to have balanced my strength and kept me straight; the two forces not being in equilibrium made my course swerve from the straight line'.

210. Samson's ascription of his fall to defect of wisdom sounds like a reflection on the Almighty, who portioned out his wisdom to him.

212. pretend they ne'er so wise, be their intentions ne'er so wise.

219-227. Cf. *Judges*, xiv., xv. 1-6.

219. Timna, or Timnath, a village of Philistia, near to Gath.

223. intimate impulse, impulse in my inmost (Lat. *intimus*) heart, in the depths of my heart.

therefore is to be taken in connection with 'that I might begin'.

227-233. Cf. *Judges*, xvi. 4.

229. Dalila. Scanned throughout the play *Dálĭla*, and so, too, in *Paradise Lost*, ix. 1060, 1061:

> "the harlot-lap
> Of Philistean Dalilah".

231. from, in accordance with.

235. a peal of words. The metaphor appears to be from a peal of artillery cannonading a 'fort'. Cf. the 'tongue-batteries' of line 404. Verity quotes Milton's *Reason of Church Government*, ii.: "to profess, to petition, and never leave pealing our ears".

236. Observe that Samson's contempt is for women as women, and not merely for Dalila among women.

241, sqq. Masson suggests "an occult reference perhaps to the conduct of those in power in England after Cromwell's death, when Milton still argued vehemently against the restoration of the Stuarts".

244. Singly by me, an inversion, 'by my unaided hand'.

249. persisted deaf, persisted in their deafness. Cf. Essay on Milton's English, § 5 (*c*).

251-264. Cf. *Judges*, xv. 8-17.

253. Etham, a village of Judah, near Zora and Eshtaol.

was retired. We make 'retire' a neuter verb; the Elizabethans made it transitive = 'remove'.

263. a trivial weapon, the jaw-bone of an ass, of which the same phrase is used in line 142.

267. lorded over, been lords over. Cf. Essay on Milton's English, § 3 (a) i.

268. The verb is omitted. Cf. Essay on Milton's English, § 5 (c).

271. Another instance in which the idea of one line is dwelt upon and elaborated in a second. Cf. note on line 18.

273. Whom, for 'him whom'. Cf. line 150, note.

277–289. It is a frequent function of the Greek chorus to illustrate the immediate story of the play by reference to similar situations in other familiar legends.

277–281. Cf. *Judges*, viii. 5–9. Gideon was in pursuit of Zebah and Zalmunna, kings of Midian, when the towns of Succoth and Penuel refused to give his warriors bread.

281. Madian. This is the Septuagint form of the Authorized Version Midian.

282–289. Cf. *Judges*, xii. 1–6. The men of Ephraim were wrath with Jephthah for fighting the Ammonites without them. He defeated them and slew them, knowing them by their inability to say the word 'Shibboleth', for the men of Ephraim said 'Sibboleth'.

283. Had, the subjunctive, now more usually 'would have'.

by argument. The arguments addressed by Jephthah to the Ammonites in *Judges*, xi. 15–27 were good, but not efficacious, "The king of the children of Ammon hearkened not unto the words of Jephthah".

291. mine, my people.

The First Stasimon.—Lines 293-329.

The Chorus now sums up the past scene with reflections on the inscrutableness of the workings of God. It was his will, for some end of his own, that Samson should marry the Philistine woman. This helps to prepare us for an end of the play, other than can be yet foreseen.

The choric odes, other than the πάροδος, were known as Stasima (στάσιμα) or 'stationary songs', *i.e.* songs sung not as marches, but after the Chorus had taken up its station in the orchestra. They were accompanied by rhythmic dance movements.

293, 294. Cf. Milton's announcement of his intention at the beginning of *Paradise Lost*, i. 24–26 :

"That, to the highth of this great argument,
I may assert Eternal Providence,
And justify the ways of God to men".

295. The antecedent is again omitted. Cf. lines 150, 273.

think not God, think God not to exist. Verity suggests that the construction is a Greek one, and quotes Plato, *Apology*, 18 C: "οἱ γὰρ ἀκούοντες ἡγοῦνται τοὺς ταῦτα ζητοῦντας οὐδὲ θεοὺς νομίζειν". ('The hearers think that those who seek these things do not even believe gods [to exist]'.)

297. 'No school or sect of philosophers ever deliberately professed Atheism.'

298. Cf. *Psalms*, xiv. 1: "The fool hath said in his heart, There is no God".

299. doctor, in the general sense of 'learned disputant in the schools'.

301. edicts. Scan *edicts'*, and cf. Essay on Metre, § 10.

307. the Interminable, *i.e.* the Infinite, he who is not bound by any limit. (Lat. *terminus* or *finis*.)

312. national obstriction, the obligation on a Jew not to marry outside his own nation. The argument of the Chorus is: God was entitled to exempt Samson from this obligation, and to allow his marriage with Dalila, in order to bring about the deliverance of Israel. But how did Samson's marriage work to this end? This point the Chorus do not tackle, for they are interrupted by the arrival of Manoa. In the Bible, Samson's first marriage is said to be of God (*Judges*, xiv. 4), but this is not said of his second.

313. legal debt, that is, debt or obligation to the Mosaic law.

319. The Nazarite vow, as laid down in *Numbers*, vi., makes no special reference to marriage, though doubtless it would be against the spirit of it to touch that unclean thing, the daughter of a Philistine.

320. fallacious, in the literal sense of the Latin *fallax*, deceitful.

322. *i.e.* 'Accept the decree of God, without submitting it to human reasoning'.

323–325. This clause is an afterthought, not referring to line 322, but modifying the 'unchaste' of line 321. Dalila was from the beginning 'unclean', *i.e.* prohibited by the Mosaic law; only unchaste after she deceived Samson. Her unchastity is rather inferred from than stated in *Judges*, xvi. 4–20. There is nothing to identify her with the 'harlot' of verse 1. Milton repeats the charge in *Paradise Lost*, ix. 1059–1062:

> "So rose the Danite strong,
> Herculean Samson, from the harlot-lap
> Of Philistean Dalila, and waked
> Shorn of his strength".

Cf. also lines 532–540. But there is an inconsistency throughout in Milton's view of Dalila. Here and in the 'spousal embraces' of line 389 and the 'marriage-choices' of line 420, as well as in the

scene where she appears, he treats her as Samson's wife: in the
Paradise Lost passage, and in lines 532–540 as a harlot or concubine.
She is not called a wife in the Bible. It is, in any case, Milton's
object to lay stress on Samson's 'sensual sin' as the cause of his fall.

328. advise, consider. Cf. Glossary.

The Second Episode.—Lines 330–651.

Further emphasis is laid upon Samson's sin—the revelation of his
secret to the 'venereal trains' of Dalila; and at last a start is made
with the action proper, with Manoa's reference to Dagon's triumph
(line 433), and announcement of his intention to try and secure his
son's liberty. Cf. lines 481, 601. With this last motive begins
the irony of the play, for Samson's liberty will be secured in a very
different fashion.

Lines 606–651 form a second μονῳδία. Cf. note on lines 1–114.

330. another inward grief. Samson's pity for the aged father
bereft of his son.

332. men of Dan. Manoa and Samson were of this tribe. Cf.
Judges, xiii. 2.

333. uncouth, strange, it being unnatural for Israelites to be
found in Philistia. Cf. Glossary, s.v.

334. gloried, for the formation of the participle from a noun, cf.
Essay on Milton's English, § 3 (*a*) i.

345. Cf. *Judges*, xv. 15.

348. At one spear's length; "which", says Mr. Verity, "would
give him room to escape the blind Samson". But then what is the
point of 'armed'? I think there are two points compressed into
the phrase: (1) Samson could not escape, if within reach of an
enemy's spear; (2) *one* spear is opposed to the 'armies' of line 345.
That is to say 'one' belongs to 'spear', not to 'length'.

349. The verb is omitted, the sense being, 'what in man is not
deceivable and vain?' Cf. Essay on Milton's English, § 5 (*c*).

352, 353. barrenness In wedlock: cf. *Judges*, xiii. 2.

354. as; the more usual conjunction is 'that'.

363–365. glorious...Ensnared...&c. The epithets belong to the
noun-idea of 'Samson', taken out of 'thy nurture' and 'a plant'.

364. miracle, subject for wonder. Cf. Glossary.

373. Cf. the sentiment of line 210.

377. profaned, made public, revealed (lit. spoken forth, the
Lat. *profari*), the usual word used in speaking of pagan religious
mysteries, and so here of the secret entrusted by God to Samson.

380. A Canaanite. The Philistines are roughly classed with the
other non-Israelite tribes of Canaan.

381. This, *i.e.* that a Canaanite woman would be my faithless
enemy.

382-387. Cf. *Judges*, xiv. 10-19.

387. **this other**, Dalila.

389. **Spousal embraces.** These words are in apposition to 'her prime of love'.

390. **Though offer'd only**: cf. *Judges*, xvi. 5.

392. **Thrice.** The three attempts are detailed in *Judges*, xvi. 6-9, 10-12, 13-14 respectively.

394. **capital.** Professor Masson considers that the word is used in the double sense of (*a*) chief, (*b*) concerning my head (L. *caput*). This seems to me rather too much of a pun for Milton. I should be content with the first sense. The same doubt arises in *Paradise Lost*, xii. 383, 384: " Needs must the Serpent now his capital bruise Expect".

404. **Tongue-batteries.** Cf. line 235, note.

410. **effeminacy.** Again the key-note of Samson's sin is touched.

414-419. Mr. Verity quotes Hall, *Contemplations*, x. 4: " He was more blind when he saw licentiously, than now when he sees not. He was a greater slave when he served his affections, than now in grinding for the Philistines."

417. These piled-up negative adjectives are characteristic of Milton's style. Cf. :

" Unrespited, unpitied, unreprieved" (*P. L.*, ii. 185).
" Unprevented, unimplored, unsought" (*P. L.*, iii. 231).
" Immutable, immortal, infinite" (*P. L.*, iii. 373).
" Unshaken, unseduced, unterrified " (*P. L.*, v. 899).
"Defaced, deflowered, and now to death devote" (*P. L.*, ix. 901).

Similar collocations may be found in earlier poets; thus in Spenser's *Faerie Queene*, vii. 7. 46:

"Unbodied, unsoul'd, unheard, unseen ";

and Daniel's *Civil Wars*, ii. 52:

" Uncourted, unrespected, unobeyed ".

Much finer, to my mind, is the varied cadence of Shakespeare's *Hamlet*, i. 5. 77:

' Unhouselled, disappointed, unaneled '.

It is, however, from the Greek tragic poets that the tradition of such lines comes. Cf. Aesch. *Agamemnon*, 666:

ἑλέναυς, ἕλανδρος, ἑλέπτολις

(' Ship's Hell, Man's Hell, City's Hell ', tr. Browning);

and Soph. *Antigone*, 876:

ἄκλαυτος, ἄφιλος, ἀνυμέναιος

(' unwept, unfriended, unbridegroomed ').

420–423. Cf. *Judges*, xiv. 1–4, where Samson's only expressed argument is 'for she likes me well'.

424. state, dwelt upon, discuss. Cf. Glossary.

433–445. At last the real action of the play begins. Manoa dwells on the triumph of Dagon; and this is the first thing that urges Samson to his great deed.

439. slew'st them many a slain. Cf. *Judges*, xvi. 24. 'Them' = 'to their hurt', an ethic dative. The phrase 'to slay a slain' is curious. Mr. Verity finds it imitated in Dryden's *Alexander's Feast*: "Thrice he routed all his foes, and thrice he slew the slain". But the sense here is quite different. Alexander "fought all his battles o'er again", and slew the slain once more in imagination.

440. magnified, glorified.

446. with shame, used as an adj. = 'shameful'.

453. idolists = idolaters, not found elsewhere; but in *Paradise Regained*, iv. 234, Milton has *idolisms* in the different sense of 'prejudices' or 'preconceptions', the *idola* of Bacon's *Novum Organum*.

454. diffidence, want of trust; now used only in the special sense of want of trust in oneself.

457. Which. The antecedent is formed by the whole of what Samson has just confessed.

460. only, an adjective, 'sole'.

461. With me, so far as I am concerned.

463. Me overthrown. The absolute participial clause is a characteristic Latinism. Cf. Essay on Milton's English, § 6 (*a*).

465. He, the God of Abraham.

468–471. Samson must not be supposed to know as yet the nature of the discomfit Dagon is to receive. That first dawns upon him in lines 1381–1383.

470. on, over, a common use.

474. Nothing more certain, to be taken as a parenthetic clause —'nothing is more certain'.

483. There is nothing said about any possible ransom of Samson in the Book of *Judges*.

486. Yet Samson was still to do them the greatest harm of his life.

496, 497. The early editions read:

> " *The mark of fool set on his front,*
> *But I God's counsel have not kept, his holy secret*".

One can hardly doubt that the alteration, made by later editors in the interests of the metre, is correct.

499-501. The allusion seems to be to the Greek myth of Tantalus, punished in Tartarus for betraying the secrets of Zeus. Cf. Ovid, *Ars Amatoria*, ii. 605:

> *O bene, quod, frustra captatis arbore pomis,*
> *Garrulus in media Tantalus aret aqua!*

501. their Abyss, the abyss of Tartarus, they believe in.

503. act not in thy own affliction, 'Do not actively help to afflict thyself'. 'In'='in the matter of'.

514. argues over-just. The Latin use of *arguere* (to prove), with an adjective.

516. what offer'd means, *i.e.* those offered means which; Keightley somewhat needlessly puts a full stop at 'means', and makes the rest of the sentence an interrogation.

517. But=other than that. Cf. *Paradise Lost*, x. 787, 788:

> "who knows
> But I shall die a living death?"

528. The sons of Anak. Cf. line 148, note.

531. my affront, my encounter, in the literal sense of the Latin *ad frontem*, to the face.

535, 536. pledge Of all my strength, *i.e.* his hair.

537. concubine, Dalila. Cf. note on lines 323-325.

shore me. The ethic dative, used with verbs of advantage or disadvantaging.

541-557. Samson's sensuality in the matter of women is compared with his temperance in the matter of wine. Abstinence from wine was part of the definite Nazarite vow. Cf. *Judges*, xiii. 7.

543. the…ruby, the colour of the red wine. Cf. *Paradise Lost*, v. 633, 634:

> "rubied nectar flows
> In pearl, in diamond, and in massy gold".

dancing, alluding to the brightness of wine when poured. Cf. *Proverbs*, xxiii. 31: "Look not thou upon the wine when it is red, when it giveth his colour in the cup, when it moveth itself aright".

545. A curious instance of the mixture of scriptural and pagan in Milton's thought. In *Psalms*, civ. 15, we have "wine that maketh glad the heart of man", and in *Judges*, ix. 13, "wine, which cheereth God and man"; but Milton, with the feasts of Olympus in his mind, turns 'God' into 'gods'.

547-549. Professor Percival points out that springs flowing eastward were supposed to have special health-giving properties. He quotes *Ezekiel*, xlvii. 1, 8, 9, and Burton, *Anatomy of Melancholy*, ii. 2, i. 1: "Rain-water is purest…next to it fountain-water that riseth in the east, and runneth eastward, from a quick running spring".

549. Cf. Euripides, *Supplices*, 652:

λαμπρὰ μὲν ἀκτὶς ἡλίου, κανὼν σαφὴς
ἔβαλλε γαῖαν

('a bright ray of the sun, a clear rod, smote the earth').

550. **the clear milky juice**, an extraordinary periphrasis for water as opposed to 'the juice of the grape'. But it is Milton's chief defect as a poet that he does not describe natural things 'with his eye on the object'. Cf. *Paradise Lost*, v. 305, 306:

" not disrelish thirst
Of nectarous draughts between, from milky stream".

It is perhaps worth noting that Milton himself seldom drank wine.

553–557. This rebuke is obviously less dramatic than didactic, intended for the roisterers of the Restoration.

557. **the liquid brook.** All drinks are liquid, but the sense here is that of the Latin *liquidus*, clear.

559. **another object**, *i.e.* woman.

562. **Effeminately.** The word is derived from *femina*, a woman, and generally means 'like a woman'; here it is possibly rather 'by a woman'.

566. **But to sit idle.** This long clause is not very logically attached to the principal sentence; to sit idle is not a way of serving the nation. It really depends on the general idea of 'What can I do?' taken out of the principal clause.

567. **a gaze.** Cf. note to line 34.

568–570. **these...strength.** The whole of this is an absolute participial clause. Cf. Milton's English, § 6 (*a*).

568. **redundant**, in the radical sense of 'flowing'.

581–583. Cf. *Judges*, xv. 18, 19, where 'the jaw' should probably be 'the rock', *i.e.* Lehi, the rock shaped like a jaw-bone. Cf. note to line 145.

586. **I persuade me so**, I assure myself that this will be so.

591. **treat**, have to do with.

593. **double darkness**, *i.e.* blindness and death.

594–596. Cf. *Hamlet*, i. 2. 133:

" How weary, stale, flat, and unprofitable
Seem to me all the uses of this world!"

600. **humours black.** The old physiology regarded the moods and temperaments as due to the preponderance of certain 'humours' in the blood. Thus 'melancholy' is literally 'black bile' (Gk. μέλας χολή). Cf. Burton, *Anatomy of Melancholy*: "The spirits being darkened, and the substance of the brain cloudy and dark, all the objects thereof appear terrible, and the mind itself, by those dark,

obscure, gross fumes, ascending from black humours, is in continual darkness, fear, and sorrow".

603. prosecute, in the sense of the Latin *prosequor*, pursue.

604. how else, by any other means.

612, 613. his...her. Cf. Glossary, s.v. *her*.

615. answerable, *i.e.* corresponding to the physical pains just spoken of.

623. deadly stings. For the metaphor, cf. lines 19–21.

627. medicinal. The word is printed *med'cinal* in the first edition, but may either be pronounced, I think, *médiçinal* or *médicinal*. Cf. Essay on Metre, § 8 (ii) *d*.

628. Alp, said to be used as a synonym for 'mountain'; and the editors quote *Paradise Lost*, ii. 620: "many a frozen, many a fiery Alp". But 'snowy' seems to be a reminiscence of the Alps proper, which Milton must have seen from Italy.

629–631. The curious musical effect of the imperfect triple rhyme *O'er...cure...despair* should be noted.

645. repeated, made again and again.

648. Scan *evils* and *remediless*, and cf. Essay on Metre, § 8 (ii) *e*.

The Second Stasimon.—Lines 652–724.

The Chorus begin upon the note of sympathy with Samson's monody. How hollow are all philosophical consolations (652–666). They then marvel at the instability which the will of God attaches to human fortunes (667–704), and pray for some better end for Samson (705–709). Here they break off, to announce the approach of Dalila (710–724).

655. to the bearing well. Possibly this may be governed by 'consolatories writ', and 'to' may = 'with a view to'; but I think it is more likely governed by the idea of 'exhorting', taken from 'extolling'. If so, 'consolatories' is in apposition to 'sayings'.

657. Consolatories, books of consolation. Probably Milton had especially in mind the famous treatise *De Consolatione Philosophiae* of the late Latin writer, Boethius.

658. sought. The participle is used as an adjective to 'persuasion'.

659. Lenient. Here, on the contrary, the adjective is used as what it is etymologically, a participle or verbal noun. The sense is 'a lenitive', 'that which soothes', from the Lat. *lenire*. The editors quote Horace, *Epist.* i. 1. 34:

> " Sunt verba et voces, quibus hunc lenire dolorem
>   Possis".

662. of dissonant mood, out of keeping with. The metaphor is musical, from a tune that does not harmonize with a given state of emotion. 'Dissonant' = 'sounding amiss': 'mood' = a *modus* or style of music. Cf. *Lycidas*, 87:

"That strain I heard was of a higher mood";

and *Paradise Lost*, i. 550–553:

"the Dorian mood
Of flutes and soft recorders; such as raised
To highth of noblest temper heroes old
Arming to battle".

The Greeks distinguished the Ionian and Lydian moods, which were sensuous, the Phrygian, which was frenzied, and the Dorian, which was moderate or ethical.

667. what is Man? Cf. *Psalms*, viii. 4: "What is man, that thou art mindful of him? and the son of man, that thou visitest him?"

672. The angelic orders. The mediaeval belief as to angels is given most fully in the *De Caelesti Hierarchia* of the pseudo-Dionysius the Areopagite. Here they are divided into three groups, each containing three orders. These are Seraphim, Cherubim, and Thrones; Dominations, Virtues, and Powers; Principalities, Archangels, and Angels.

676. the summer-fly, the insects known as *Ephemeridae*, the creatures of a day (ἐπί, ἡμέρα). So Hamlet of Osric (*Hamlet*, v. 2. 82): "Dost know this water-fly?"

683. highth. This appears to be Milton's deliberate spelling, and is as such retained.

686. 'A request of service from them to thee.'

690. Unseemly falls. This is in apposition to the whole idea conveyed in the preceding sentence. Cf. Milton's English, § 8.

693, 694. their carcasses...a prey. Cf. Homer, *Iliad*, i. 4:

αὐτοὺς δὲ ἑλώρια τεῦχε κύνεσσιν
οἰωνοῖσί τε πᾶσιν.

('And them he made a prey for dogs and for every bird').

694. or else captived. This is co-ordinate with 'to the hostile sword', the clause 'their carcasses...a prey' being an absolute one. Cf. Milton's English, § 6 (*a*).

695. change of times. Milton is speaking very directly now of his own fate at the Restoration. It may be remembered that the bodies of Cromwell, Bradshaw, and Ireton were disinterred and hanged, that Vane was executed after a most partial trial, and that Lambert was also tried and imprisoned for life in Guernsey.

702, 703. 'Though their lives have not been disorderly, yet without cause they suffer the punishment which belongs to the dissolute.'

710–724. This elaborate description of the sumptuous appearance of Dalila is meant to emphasize the contrast between her fate and that of the broken-down world-weary Samson in his prison garb.

714. a stately ship. We often speak of a woman 'sailing in'. Todd quotes a similar description of prelates in full canonicals from *Reformation in England*: "under sail in all their lawn and sarcenet, their shrouds and tackle".

715. Of Tarsus. The 'ships of Tarshish' are frequently mentioned in the Bible; but Tarshish was probably the Phoenician Tartessus in Spain, not Tarsus in Cilicia.

715, 716. the isles Of Javan, the Biblical name for Greece. Javan = Ιάων, the father of the Ionians. Cf. *Isaiah*, lxvi. 19: "I will send those that escape of them unto the nations, to Tarshish…and Javan, to the isles far off".

716. Gadire, the Gk. Γάδειρα, the Latin *Gades*, the modern *Cadiz*.

719. hold them play, hold play *for* them.

720, 721. Another absolute construction.

722. Mr. Verity points out that Dalila is not stated to have been a Philistine in the Bible, though it is natural to suppose she was.

Third Episode.—Lines 725–1009.

Dalila addresses Samson with feigned humility, expresses penitence (732–747), blames Samson himself (766–818), excuses herself (843–870), attempts a reconciliation (907–927), and finding Samson obdurate, finally triumphs over him (960–996).

This is perhaps the most dramatic scene in the play. The contrast between the smooth, specious, intriguing woman and her stern judge, inflexible in suffering, is finely drawn. And Dalila's final assertion of the Philistine point of view lends a variety of interest which the somewhat monotonous recital of Samson's misfortunes has hitherto excluded from the play.

726. fix'd, fixedly; adjective for adverb. Cf. Milton's English, § 3 (*a*) iii.

727. with head declined. The name Dalila signifies 'the bowing or drooping one'.

736, 737. more evil…than I foresaw. This is not borne out by *Judges*, xvi. 5. Probably Dalila is meant to be playing the hypocrite throughout the scene up to line 960.

742. of, concerning.

743. in my ability, that I am able to do.

748. hyaena. The hyaena was supposed to shed tears, and to imitate the human voice, thus leading men to destruction. Cf. the passage from Bartholomew Anglicus in Steele's *Mediaeval Lore*, p. 130: "And herds tell that among stables, he feigneth speech of mankind, and calleth some man by his own name, and rendeth him when he hath him without "; also Ben Jonson, *Volpone*, iv. 2:

> " Out, thou chamaeleon harlot ! Now thine eyes
> Vie tears with the hyaena ".

749–765. Milton was reconciled to his first wife, after two years separation, in 1645. The event is thus described by Phillips: " On a sudden he was surprised to see one whom he thought to have never seen more, making submission, and begging pardon on her knees before him.... His...generous nature...and...the strong intercession of friends on both sides...soon brought him to an act of oblivion and firm league of peace for the future ". As to the after-result of this experiment in Milton's case we know little.

755. ' How far his patience will bear urging.'

759. **That,** so that.

763. a poisonous bosom-snake. The fable, found in Aesop and elsewhere, of the countryman who warmed a frozen snake in his bosom and was stung by it, affords a ready type of ingratitude. Cf. Shakespeare, *Richard II.*, iii. 2. 131: " Snakes, in my heart-blood warm'd, that sting my heart ".

764. cut off, suddenly destroyed: a common Biblical phrase.

770. counterpoised should be taken with ' aggravations ' rather than with ' it '. ' If the circumstances which aggravate the offence are to be taken into consideration, so also should those which extenuate it.'

773–777. One of Milton's loose-jointed sentences: *Curiosity...to publish...female faults* are all constructed in apposition to *a weakness*.

776. like infirmity. Too great readiness to tell is like too great eagerness to learn.

782. But introduces a supposed reply of Samson's to the preceding argument.

795. her at Timna. Cf. *Judges*, xiv. 19, 20.

796. to endear, to make myself dear to thee.

800. ' Why then I revealed them.'

800–802. Another lie. Cf. *Judges*, xvi. 5.

803. made for me, helped to bring about my object.

809. Whole, wholly.

810. The construction is changed. ' Fearless ', though rhythmically parallel to ' whole ' and ' unhazarded ', must be grammatically joined with ' myself ', not ' thee '.

820. upbraid me mine. The more usual idiom is ' upbraid me with mine '; but here ' upbraid me ' seems to be equivalent to a single verb, such as ' blame ', and to govern ' mine '.

826. **which.** The grammatical subject is strictly 'pardon', but according to the sense it is rather the mental attitude which in Milton takes the place of pardon towards himself, *i.e.* self-condemnation.

836. **But love constrain'd thee.** Here, as in line 782, by a common rhetorical device, the speaker puts an argument in the mouth of his opponent.

840. The construction is a Latinism. Cf. Milton's English, § 5 (*b*).

843. 'Since thou decidest weakness to be no plea.'

844. 'Though this decision implies the condemnation of thyself.'

848. **The constantest.** For the somewhat unusual form of the superlative, cf. Milton's English, § 3 (*b*).

850. Cf. *Judges*, xvi. 5, 18, from which we gather that it *was* gold.

856. **A common enemy,** an enemy to the community.

857. **the priest.** Milton, the sturdy Independent, has no love for the professional minister of religion. Cf. lines 1419, 1420.

865. **grounded,** firmly grounded, built on secure foundations, well established.

870. Another absolute participial clause.

871. **circling,** beating round and round the truth without actually touching it.

879. **Too well.** This is not a repetition of the 'too well' of the previous line, but goes with 'loved thee'.

881. **who could.** The relative, far separated from its antecedent 'I', in line 876, stands for a causal clause: 'Since I could deny thee nothing'.

885. Cf. *Genesis*, ii. 24: "Therefore shall a man leave his father and his mother, and shall cleave unto his wife".

887. **their,** the Philistines'.

888. **mine, not theirs.** It is a little ambiguous whether 'mine' ='my subject', or 'under my protection': perhaps both.

893. **the ends,** that is, the preservation of family life in peace, whereas the Philistines were trying to break up a family.

895. Cf. note to line 836.

900. **Less,** that is, less even than the name of country.

901. An absolute participial construction.

904. **Goes by the worse,** gets the worst of it.

905. Ironically spoken.

906. **thy peals.** Cf. note to line 235.

908. **would have succeeded best,** would have had the best success, issue, or event.

912. **Misguided,** either a verb in apposition to 'misdone', or a participle used as an adjective to 'I'.

915. enjoy'd goes with 'Life', not 'solaces'.

921. Their favourable ear, that their ear will be favourable.

927. what, *i.e.* sight.

934. There seems to be a reference in the 'enchanted cup' to the classical story of Circe, and in 'warbling charms' to that of the Sirens.

936. Cf. *Psalms*, lviii. 4, 5: "They are like the deaf adder that stoppeth her ear: Which will not hearken to the voice of charmers, charming never so wisely": cf. also the counsel of Scripture: "Be ye wise as serpents, harmless as doves".

945. uxorious to, submissive to, as a man who is governed by his wife.

955–959. Note the tone of bitter sarcasm with which Samson dismisses Dalila.

960–996. A fine speech, in an impassioned strain, contrasting with the frigid rhetoric of the rest of the scene.

967. Bid, a participle, 'bidden to go'.

evil omen, in the curse invoked upon her by Samson in the form of a blessing. Cf. lines 955–959.

971–974. A passage of ornament and metaphor, such as occur rarely in the play. The description of Fame is partly taken from Chaucer's *House of Fame*, bk. iii., where Fame is accompanied by 'dan Eolus' as a trumpeter, with a 'blakke trumpe of bras' which is 'y-cleped Slaunder' and a 'trumpe of golde' that is 'highte Laude'. But the precise description here given is Milton's own, suggested, as line 971 shows, by the Roman 'two-faced Janus'. Silius Italicus, in the *Punica*, xv. 95, &c., introduces Infamy as a black-winged goddess, Glory and Victory as white-winged goddesses; and *Fama Bona* is white-winged in Ben Jonson's *Masque of Queens*. In Virgil, *Aeneid*, iv. 181, 182, Fame is winged, and each feather covers an eye, and Rumour is similarly described by Shakespeare in *2 Henry IV.*, *Induction*. Milton again borrows from Chaucer in the description of Fame in his Latin poem *In Quintum Novembris*. Of course the point of Milton's description is that the trumpets blowing in opposite directions, and the differently coloured wings, symbolize the fact that what to some hearers seems infamous, to others seems glorious.

972. with contrary blast, that is, with blasts from both his trumpets, which point in contrary directions.

975. the Circumcised, the Jews, as distinguished from the Philistines. Cf. note on line 144.

979. most unconjugal, most unworthy of a wife.

981. Ecron, Gaza, Asdod, Gath. Four of the great cities of Philistia, Ascalon being the fifth.

982-984. Cf. Euripides, *Herakleidai*, 597, 598:

πασῶν γυναικῶν, ἴσθι, τιμιωτάτη
καὶ ζῶσ' ὑφ' ἡμῶν καὶ θανοῦσ' ἔσει πολύ

('Know this, that both living and dead thou shalt be held by us the most honourable by far of all women').

982. famousest. Cf. line 848, 'constantest', and note.

984. who, as one who, in close connection with 'recorded'.

985. chose governs the clause 'to...destroyer'.

987. odours. Cf. *Jeremiah*, xxxiv. 5: "Thou shalt die in peace: and with the burnings of thy fathers...shall they burn odours for thee".

988-990. Cf. *Judges*, iv. 17-22.

1008. There is a reference to the well-known line of Terence, *Andria*, iii. 3. 23: *Amantium irae amoris integratio est.*

The Third Stasimon.—Lines 1010-1060.

The Chorus, moralizing on the scene of which they have been spectators, sing of the imperfectness of women, the rarity of good wives, and the necessity of the man being master in his house.

1016. thy riddle. Cf. line 1064, and *Judges*, xiv. 12-19.

1018. these, the qualities enumerated in lines 1010, 1011.

1020. Thy paranymph, 'best man'. Cf. Glossary, and *Judges*, xiv. 20; xv. 2. But in the Bible the woman was given to Samson's companion after he left her. As in the case of Dalila (cf. note on lines 323-325), the charge of unfaithfulness is Milton's addition.

1022. both, the two wives.

1025. for that, because.

1027. for haste, through haste.

1030. oftest. Cf. line 848, note.

1037, 1038. a thorn Intestine. Milton has in mind *2 Cor.*, xii. 7: "there was given to me a thorn in the flesh", together with *Genesis*, ii. 24: "they shall be one flesh".

1038. within defensive arms. No armour can defend a man from the wife of his bosom.

1039. cleaving, clinging. Here again Milton makes ironical reference to *Genesis*, ii. 24: "A man shall...cleave unto his wife". The commentators find also an allusion to the clinging shirt soaked in the poisonous blood of the centaur Nessus given to Hercules by his wife Deianeira.

1048. 'That unites with her husband in preserving a virtuous household.'

1050-1052. The virtue of a man in spite of his wife is higher than that of the man who has a good wife.

1053-1060. Milton's view of the proper relations of man and wife is based upon his own unfortunate experience of women, and on *Genesis*, iii. 16: " Thy desire shall be to thy husband, and he shall rule over thee ". This is expounded in many passages of *P.L.*, *e.g.* iv. 634-638:

> " To whom thus Eve, with perfect beauty adorn'd :—
> My author and disposer, what thou bidd'st
> Unargued I obey.   So God ordains :
> God is thy law, thou mine : to know no more
> Is woman's happiest knowledge, and her praise."

The Fourth Episode.—Lines 1061-1267.

To Dalila succeeds Harapha of Gath. Samson proves as obdurate to threats and violence as to honeyed wiles. He challenges the giant to fight, who departs crest-fallen, leaving Samson much roused and in no patient mood. Dramatically this is the object of the interviews both with Dalila and Harapha, which hardly advance the action, to work up Samson into a fit temper for his great enterprise.

1062. Samson takes the word ' storm ' literally.

1064. Cf. note to line 1016.

1068. Harapha.   The name appears to be a variant of Rapha, and to be taken from a period of history later than that of Samson. In *2 Samuel*, xxi. 15-22, Rapha is the marginal reading where the text of the A.V. has simply ' the giant '.   Rapha was the father of Ishbi-benob, Saph, Goliath, and two others.

1076. condole, lament in sympathy. We use the idiom to condole *with*; but cf. *Hen. V.*, ii. 1. 133: " Let us condole the knight ".

1077. it, thy chance.

1078. no friendly intent.   Harapha means that he would have liked to measure his strength with an unvanquished Samson.

1080. Og, king of Bashan, ' of the remnant of the giants ', defeated by the Israelites at Edrei.   Cf. *Numbers*, xxi. 33-35; *Deuteronomy*, iii. 1-11.

Anak. Cf. note on line 148.

Emims. The Emims of Shaveh Kiriathaim were smitten by Chedorlaomer (*Genesis*, xiv. 5). The Israelites passed by their land. Cf. *Deuteronomy*, ii. 10, 11: " The Emims dwelt therein in times past, a people great, and many, and tall, as the Anakims; Which also were accounted giants, as the Anakims; but the Moabites call them Emims". But the Emim—the Hebrew plural ends in -*im* not -*ims* —were not identical with the Anakim, as Milton seems to imply.

1082. If thou at all art known. Cf. the boast of Satan to Zephon and Ithuriel in *P.L.*, iv. 830: " Not to know me argues yourself unknown".

1088. Note the omission of the demonstrative.

1094. **the field** of Ramath-Lechi. Cf. lines **142–145**, and notes.

1100. **the unforeskinn'd race**, the circumcised Jews.

1101. **honour** is used as the object both to 'to have won' and 'I lose'.

1102. **mortal duel**, duel to the death.

1105. **in thy hand**, in thy power. Samson's point is, 'You have now the opportunity you say you wish you had had before'.

1107. This taunt, intended as an insult to the slave, strikes one as bathos.

1108, 1109. There is no principal sentence; we may suppose 'Such usage' to be in apposition with or explanatory of the idea of squalor, suggested by Harapha's last remark.

1116. **feign'd shifts.** Samson's criticism on lines 1106, 1107.

1118. **flight.** The rhyme with 'sight' in the preceding line points the jeer.

1119–1123. The irony is suggested by the contrast of the armed Goliath and the unarmed David in *1 Samuel*, xvii. 4–7, 43, Goliath "had an helmet of brass upon his head; and he was armed with a coat of mail....he had greaves of brass upon his legs, and a target of brass between his shoulders. And the staff of his spear was like a weaver's beam; and his spear's head weighed six hundred shekels of iron". David came to him, as Samson would to Harapha, 'with staves'.

1122. **A weaver's beam**, the wooden roller on which the yarn to be woven in a loom is rolled. I suppose it is the 'pin of the web', mentioned in *Judges*, xvi. 14.

seven-times-folded, the ἐπταβόειον σάκος ('shield seven ox-hides thick') of Homer, translated in Virgil, *Aeneid*, vi. 220: "clipei septemplicis orbis".

1124. **outcries.** There seems to be some confusion of idea between the clatter of blows on the armour and the outcries which the wounded giant will probably raise.

1130–1134. Protection in battle by spells is a notion of mediaeval romance, but there is no allusion to such a belief among the Philistines in the Biblical account of Samson.

1134. **which**, the antecedent is 'strength', taken from the preceding words 'charmed the strong'.

1138. **ruffled porcupines.** Cf. *Hamlet*, i. 5. 19:

> "And each particular hair to stand on end,
> Like quills upon the fretful porpentine".

1139. Todd points out that part of the ritual of a mediaeval combat in arms was an oath taken by the champions in the form, "I do swear, that I have not upon me, nor on any of the arms I shall use, words, charms, or enchantments, to which I trust for help to conquer my enemy, but that I do only trust in God, in my right, and in the strength of my body and arms".

1144. Cf. *Judges*, xvi. 17.

1164. boisterous locks, the 'redundant locks, Robustious' of lines 568, 569.

1166. so, so as.

1169. From thine, *i.e.* from thy indignity, or worthlessness. Others explain it 'from those of thy nation'.

1181. Tongue-doughty. Cf. Beaumont and Fletcher, *The Little French Lawyer*: "O brave, tongue-valiant and vain-glorious woman".

1182, 1183. Cf. *Judges*, xv. 11–13.

1185–1188. Cf. *Judges*, xiv. 19.

1201. all, the whole Philistine nation.

1204. their, their own: 'to pay Philistines with Philistine gold'.

1207. well, rightly, justly.

1208–1210. An argument put rhetorically by Samson in his opponents' mouth. Cf. note to line 782.

1210. Single, single-handed.

1217. I was to, *i.e.* 'it was for me to'; 'there my duty lay, without regard to the unworthy conduct of my fellows'.

1218. my known offence, 'the offence of which I am deeply conscious, the blabbing to a woman'. Cf. lines 195–202, &c.

1222. thrice, the threefold challenge was a custom of chivalry, and *appellant* the technical term for a challenger. Cf. Glossary; and also note on line 1139.

1224–1226. Todd quotes from Saviolo, *Of Honor and Honorable Quarrels* (1595), to the effect that traitors, freebooters, robbers, and other infamous persons "are to be refused upon challenging another man".

1227. to survey me. Cf. line 1089.

1231. Baal-zebub, the god of flies; a form of the sun-god Baal worshipped in Philistia; in *2 Kings*, i. 16, he is called "the god of Ekron".

1234. bring up thy van, *i.e.* 'begin the fight', with the innuendo, 'I am ready for an army of Haraphas'.

1236. other kind of answer, not honourable fight, but punishment from the gaoler. Cf. lines 1243, 1250–1252.

1237. baffled, another term of chivalry. Cf. Glossary.

1238. Though in these chains qualifies *I*, and *bulk without spirit vast* is in apposition to *thee*.

1242. Astaroth, the female deity of Canaan, a moon or star-goddess; the 'Diana of the Ephesians' and Aphrodite-Astarte of the Greeks.

1248, 1249. five sons...Goliah chief. Cf. line 1068, note.

1252. other, to be scanned as a monosyllable. Cf. Essay on Metre, § 8 (v).

1260. The work of many hands, *i.e.* 'work it would take many other hands to do'.

1263. to rid me hence. The gerundive infinitive qualifies 'will prove' like an adverbial clause, 'provided he rids me hence'.

1264. The worst. This may stand in apposition to 'death', but it is perhaps more characteristic of Milton to put it in apposition to the whole of the preceding sentence.

1265–1267. Another prophecy of the catastrophe.

1265. so, in the way to be stated in lines 1266, 1267.

1266. with mine, with my ruin.

The Fourth Stasimon.—Lines 1268–1307.

Samson's renewed vigour on the preceding scene leads the Chorus to reflect on the beauty of strength in the hands of a man of God. They qualify this by preaching patience to Samson. There is dramatic irony in this, just at the moment when Samson is no longer called upon to exercise patience.

1277. He, not 'God', but the 'deliverer'.

1292. Either; perhaps to be taken in the sense of 'both'. Samson has been the 'deliverer'; he is now to be the patient saint. I do not think that the Chorus contemplate Samson being a deliverer in the future, though certainly the 'May chance' of 1295 favours this explanation.

1296. crown. Cf. *Revelation*, ii. 10: "Be thou faithful unto death, and I will give thee a crown of life".

The Fifth Episode.—Lines 1308–1426.

We now come to the critical action of the play. The earlier scenes were retrospective; the two last, with Dalila and Harapha, have not advanced the plot much, though we may assume that the summons of the lords to Samson is a consequence of Harapha's threat; but they have worked Samson up to the necessary pitch of physical and spiritual excitement. The present scene leads directly to Samson's great resolve, upon which the catastrophe depends.

1308. Ebrews. Milton appears to use the form *Ebrew* for the noun, *Hebrew* for the adjective.

1313. rate, printed in the first edition *race*, and corrected in the list of *Omissa*.

1320. Our law forbids. Cf. *Exodus*, xxiii. 24: "Thou shalt not bow down to their gods, nor serve them, nor do after their works; but thou shalt utterly overthrow them, and quite break down their images"; also the doubt of the convert Naaman in *2 Kings*, v. 18, whether he was justified in bowing down in the house of Rimmon.

1323-1325. A list of the popular entertainers of the Elizabethan-Jacobean age, mostly suppressed by the Puritan taste of the Long Parliament.

1324. gymnic artists, acrobats or performers of 'feats of agility'.

1333. Regard thyself, consider thy own welfare.

1334. 'My conscience and internal peace already suffer so much from my sin, that my bodily welfare affects me little.'

1338-1342. On the construction, cf. Milton's English, § 8.

1343. with speed, to be performed with speed.

1346. I am sorry is used as a transitive verb, 'I regret'.

1347. Another hint of what is coming.

1349. whether to hold or break, depends on 'the highth' in the sense of 'the deciding point'. The metaphor is from a taut rope.

1350. *i.e.* 'by exaggeration'.

1353. than, to be constructed with the adverb 'more lordly'.

1355. strength, again returning with my hair. Cf. *Judges*, xvi. 22.

1361, 1362. The clause is compressed, 'How vile, &c., and besides that, how unclean and profane'.

1369. the sentence, the maxim just quoted by the Chorus.

1375. jealousy. Milton's warrant for using the word of God is in the Fourth Commandment, *Exodus*, xx. 5: "I the Lord thy God am a jealous God".

1376. unrepented, if unrepented.

1377-1379. Cf. the case of Naaman, quoted in the note on line 1320. The limits of obedience to the civil authority was of course a much-discussed point of 17th-century casuistry.

1377. dispense with, excuse, grant a dispensation to.

1380. The Chorus give it up, as the Greek Chorus generally does when a difficult problem has to be solved.

1381-1389. Samson now makes the great resolve for which the whole course of the play has been a preparation, and of which we have had special premonitions in the lines 1265-1267. But line 1388 shows that the exact nature of what he is to do is not clear to him yet.

1382. rousing motions, obscure stirrings of the spirit to some active deed.

1390. In time, at the right moment.

1402. Because they shall not, in order that they may not.

1404, 1405. Ironically double-edged. Samson is indeed obeying a Master, but not the Philistines.

1406, 1407. This only covers Samson's real reason for his change of purpose.

1410. these links, the fetters on Samson's legs.

1418. lordliest, most overbearing.

1419. then, *i.e.* when he is well-feasted.

1419, 1420. For the attack on the priests, cf. lines 857–861.

1421. holy-days. One recalls the Puritan objection to the revelry of the wakes and other public holidays which had survived the Reformation.

1426. Loosely constructed with the rest of the sentence; the 'Whether ye may expect to hear the last of me or no I cannot warrant'.

The Fifth Stasimon.—Lines 1427-1444.

The Chorus dismisses Samson with a prayer for his success; the ode is brief, that the action once begun may not be delayed.

1431. the Angel of thy birth. Cf. *Judges*, xiii. 3–21; but the prayer implies also the mediaeval notion of a tutelary or guardian angel appointed to watch over each man during his lifetime.

1436. In the camp of Dan. Cf. *Judges*, xiii. 25.

The Exodos.—Lines 1445-1758.

The Greeks gave this name to that part of the play following the last Stasimon. Originally a play ended with an ode sung as the Chorus filed out, and this was called the ἔξοδος (ἐκ, out; ὅδος, a going). Afterwards it became customary to end a play not with a regular ode, but with a few words only from the Chorus (cf. lines 1745–1758), and then the term ἔξοδος was applied to the closing dialogue.

The Exodos of the present play is really divisible into more than one part.

(a) Lines 1445-1540. Samson leaves the stage, in obedience to the Greek rule forbidding actual deeds of violence to be enacted *coram populo.* Manoa takes his place. His hopes—full of dramatic irony—for a peaceful old age with his son, are interrupted by the noise of distant tumult.

(b) Lines 1541–1659. A Messenger enters and relates Samson's exploit and death.

(c) Lines 1660–1707. A Kommos (κόμμος) or Dirge follows, that is, a lyric sung in the course of the scene, and originally, as here, a lament for the dead. It was usual for both actors and Chorus to take part in a *Kommos*; here it is sung, partly by the Chorus as a whole, partly by the two halves of it in turn.

(d) Lines 1708–1744. Manoa sums up the tragedy in a spirit of resignation and even triumph.

(e) Lines 1745–1758. The Chorus file out, with words of a similar import.

1450. I had no will, ' to be present' is understood.

1455. Note the inversion of the natural order, ' To partake that hope would rejoice us'.

1461–1471. Masson suggests that we may find in these lines a reference to the various sections of the royalist party at the Restoration, those who "most reverenced Dagon and his priests being the extreme High-Churchmen", &c.

1464, 1465. their aim Private reward, an absolute clause.

1470. Another inversion, precisely parallel to that in line 1455, ' It was,' they said, ' magnanimity to remit the rest of their revenge'.

1490–1503. Manoa's hopes, expressed at the very moment when, to the knowledge of the audience, Samson is meeting so different a fate, is a fine example of tragic irony. The presage of lines 1495–1501 is fulfilled in a way other than the prophet expects.

1495. me, myself. The Latin *me* is used reflexively.

1501. The construction is changed; ' Samson' becomes the subject instead of 'God'.

ridiculous. In the ordinary way, the long locks of the Cavaliers were a subject of mockery to the round-headed Puritans.

1503. to, in addition to.

1507. as next, as nearest, after thee, to Samson.

1510. the former shout. Cf. line 1472.

1514. at the utmost point, to the extreme degree.

1515. ruin, that is, in the literal sense of the Latin *ruina*, a fall of buildings.

1521, 1522. The Greek Chorus is always timorous in presence of danger.

1527-1537. Lines 1527-1535 and 1537 were omitted in the first edition and line 1536 was given to the Chorus. This was corrected, or, if it was an addition, the addition was made in the list of *Omissa*, and in the second edition.

1530. There is irony again in this hope: the Chorus realize their triumph before they realize their calamity.

1537. Of good or bad. This depends on 'notice' understood from Manoa's speech. The point is 'Yes, news will come of fortune or misfortune so great as this will be; if it is of misfortune it will come the sooner'.

1549. I knew remaining. Participle for infinitive; a Latinism.

1550, 1551. As...So; equivalent to *both...and*. There does not seem to be any real antithesis.

1563. by whom, *i.e.* 'by whom fallen'.

1564, 1565. refrain...To utter. The more usual phrase is 'refrain from uttering'; 'refrain' is here used as equivalent to 'hesitate'.

1569. them, the news; properly of course a plural, but in modern English become a singular.

1570. Samson is dead. Cf. Sophocles, *Electra*, 673:

τέθνηκ' Ὀρέστης· ἐν βραχεῖ συνθεὶς λέγω

('Orestes is dead; putting the whole in brief I speak').

1571. Note that as Manoa has been unduly exultant, so now he is unduly depressed. There is an harmonious rise and fall of emotion throughout this scene.

1573. his ransom. Manoa recurs to the thought of lines 1476-1484.

1574. windy, empty, full of wind.

1576, 1577. Cf. *Love's Labour's Lost*, i. 1. 100:

"Biron is like an envious sweeping frost,
    That bites the first-born infants of the spring";

and *Henry VIII.*, iii. 2. 353-358:

"This is the state of man: to-day he puts forth
The tender leaves of hopes; to-morrow blossoms,
And bears his blushing honours thick upon him;
The third day comes a frost, a killing frost,
And when he thinks, good honest man, full surely
His greatness is a-ripening, nips his root,
And then he falls, as I do".

1594. This line is in apposition to 'thou'.

1596–1659. The long speech by a messenger, describing the catastrophe, is a very characteristic feature of Greek tragedy. It was rendered necessary by the fact that the catastrophe itself, if it consisted of a deed of violence, was not thought suitable to be brought on the stage.

1603. at, 'upon the occasion of', but we should more naturally say 'from'.

1605–1610. Cf. *Judges*, xvi. 25–30, where the building is a house with crowds on the roof. Milton describes it as a semicircular building with a vaulted roof, supported by two pillars close together in the diameter of the semicircle. Between these Samson stands; the lords sit on tiers of seats within; the people stand without, behind Samson, and clear of the roof. Mr. Verity suggests that Milton may have taken his description from the account of Gaza in the *Travels* of Sandys, who saw arches and pillars of an incredible bigness, fabled "to have been the theater of Samson, pulled down on the head of the Philistines". But it may also be noted that Milton seems to have a Greek rather than an oriental building in his mind.

1616–1619. The pageant intended for Samson's humiliation becomes his triumph.

1621. Rifted the air. Cf. the phrase in line 1472, "tore the sky".

1635. which, the pillars.

1647, 1648. Note the inversion.

1660–1707. Manoa remains silent, struggling with his sorrow, while the Chorus sing the *kommos* or dirge, half of triumph, half of lament, as is beseeming.

1661. *i.e.* 'Life or death matters little, since thou hast fulfilled'.

1665, 1666. the fold Of dire Necessity. This sounds like an echo of Greek fatalism, but it may possibly be only equivalent to the 'inevitable destruction' of lines 1657, 1658. Samson could not destroy the theatre without destroying himself.

1671. fat, adjective used as adverb.

1674. Silo, or Shiloh, where the Ark stood in Samson's time.

1675. a spirit of frenzy, the ἄτη so often spoken of in Greek tragedy, leading men on to ὕβρις or overweening pride, and thence to νέμεσις or divine retribution.

1685. reprobate is used, as in *Romans*, i. 28: "God gave them over to a reprobate mind", for the Greek ἀδόκιμος, spurious, or void of judgment. The meaning therefore is 'left to ill-judging sense'.

1692. an evening dragon, a serpent creeping after dark upon the hen-roosts.

1695. tame villatic fowl, a periphrasis for 'barn-door hens', as absurd as anything in Pope or the Popelings, who of course found in Milton the highly Latinized diction which he generally used so much more discreetly than they.

but. There is a contrast between the stealthy approach of the dragon and the sudden final swoop of the eagle.

1696. cloudless thunder, the bolt from the blue, always looked upon with superstitious dread.

1699. that self-begotten bird, the fabulous phoenix of Arabia. The following passage from Bartholomew Anglicus, quoted in Steele's *Mediaeval Lore*, will explain the allusions in lines 1699–1707: "Phoenix is a bird, and there is but one of that kind in all the wide world.... Among the Arabs—there this bird is bred—he is called singular, alone.... Phoenix...liveth three hundred or five hundred years: when the which years are past, and he feeleth his own default and feebleness, he maketh a nest of right sweet smelling sticks, that are full dry, and in summer when the western wind blows, the sticks and the nest are set on fire with burning heat of the sun, and burn strongly. Then this bird phoenix cometh wilfully into the burning nest, and is there burnt to ashes among these burning sticks, and within three days a little worm is gendered of the ashes, and waxeth little and little, and taketh feathers and is shapen and turned to a bird."

1703–1705. The phoenix was used in lines 1699–1702 as a simile for virtue; now it has become a metaphor.

1706, 1707. Virtue, rather than the bird, is now again in Milton's mind. The phoenix survives in more than mere fame.

1707. ages of lives, *i.e.* through ages of lives.

1708–1724. The opening lines of Manoa's speech, with their solemn movement and accent of almost exultant resignation, are among the finest in the play.

1713. the sons of Caphtor, the Philistines. So called from *Amos*, ix. 7: "Have not I brought up...the Philistines from Caphtor?"; *Jeremiah*, xlvii. 4: "The Lord will spoil the Philistines, the remnant of the country of Caphtor"; *Deuteronomy*, ii. 23: "the Avims which dwelt in Hazerim, even unto Azzah; the Caphtorims, which came forth out of Caphtor, destroyed them, and dwelt in their stead".

1730. Cf. *Judges*, xvi. 31.

1741–1744. A reversal of the hope of Dalila in 986, 987.

1748. This line is an epithet of 'Wisdom', co-ordinate with 'highest'.

1751. in place, 'in this present place', 'here, as we have seen'.

Cf. *Measure for Measure*, v. 504: "Here's one in place I cannot pardon".

1758. Cf. the account of the purpose of tragedy given in Milton's preface.

1745–1758. Euripides frequently ends his plays with some remarks of the Chorus to the effect of 'Inscrutable are the ways of God'. Milton varies this in the sense of Christian philosophy: 'The ways of God are past finding out, but always for the best'. The last words of the play remind one also of the blessing which concludes the Communion service of the Anglican church: "The peace of God, which passeth all understanding, keep your hearts and minds in the knowledge and love of God, and of His son Jesus Christ our Lord".

APPENDIX A.

THE BOOK OF JUDGES: Chaps. XIII.–XVI.

And the children of Israel did evil again in the sight of the Lord; and the Lord delivered them into the hand of the Philistines forty years.

And there was a certain man of Zorah, of the family of the Danites, whose name was Manoah; and his wife was barren, and bare not. And the angel of the Lord appeared unto the woman, and said unto her, Behold now, thou art barren, and bearest not: but thou shalt conceive, and bear a son. Now therefore beware, I pray thee, and drink not wine nor strong drink, and eat not any unclean thing: for, lo, thou shalt conceive, and bear a son; and no razor shall come on his head: for the child shall be a Nazarite unto God from the womb; and he shall begin to deliver Israel out of the hand of the Philistines.

Then the woman came and told her husband, saying, A man of God came unto me, and his countenance was like the countenance of an angel of God, very terrible: but I asked him not whence he was, neither told he me his name. But he said unto me, Behold, thou shalt conceive, and bear a son; and now drink no wine nor strong drink, neither eat any unclean thing: for the child shall be a Nazarite to God from the womb to the day of his death. Then Manoah entreated the Lord, and said, O my Lord, let the man of God which thou didst send come again unto us, and teach us what we shall do unto the child that shall be born. And God hearkened to the voice of Manoah; and the angel of God came again unto the woman as she sat in the field: but Manoah her husband was not with her. And the woman made haste, and ran, and showed her husband, and said unto him, Behold, the man hath appeared unto me, that came unto me the other day. And Manoah arose, and went after his wife, and came to the man, and said unto him, Art thou the man that spakest unto the woman? And he said, I am. And Manoah said,

Now let thy words come to pass: how shall we order the child? and how shall we do unto him? And the angel of the Lord said unto Manoah, Of all that I said unto the woman let her beware. She may not eat of any thing that cometh of the vine, neither let her drink wine or strong drink, nor eat any unclean thing: all that I commanded her let her observe.

And Manoah said unto the angel of the Lord, I pray thee, let us detain thee until we shall have made ready a kid for thee. And the angel of the Lord said unto Manoah, Though thou detain me, I will not eat of thy bread; and if thou wilt offer a burnt-offering, thou must offer it unto the Lord: for Manoah knew not that he was an angel of the Lord. And Manoah said unto the angel of the Lord, What is thy name, that when thy sayings come to pass we may do thee honour? And the angel of the Lord said unto him, Why askest thou thus after my name, seeing it is secret? So Manoah took a kid with a meat-offering, and offered it upon a rock unto the Lord: and the angel did wondrously; and Manoah and his wife looked on. For it came to pass, when the flame went up toward heaven from off the altar, that the angel of the Lord ascended in the flame of the altar: and Manoah and his wife looked on it, and fell on their faces to the ground. (But the angel of the Lord did no more appear to Manoah and to his wife.) Then Manoah knew that he was an angel of the Lord. And Manoah said unto his wife, We shall surely die, because we have seen God. But his wife said unto him, If the Lord were pleased to kill us, he would not have received a burnt-offering and a meat-offering at our hands; neither would he have showed us all these things; nor would, as at this time, have told us such things as these.

And the woman bare a son, and called his name Samson: and the child grew, and the Lord blessed him. And the Spirit of the Lord began to move him at times in the camp of Dan, between Zorah and Eshtaol.

And Samson went down to Timnath, and saw a woman in Timnath of the daughters of the Philistines. And he came up, and told his father and his mother, and said, I have seen a woman in Timnath of the daughters of the Philistines; now therefore get her for me to wife. Then his father and his mother said unto him, Is there never a woman among the daughters of thy brethren, or among all my people, that thou goest to take a wife of the uncircumcised Philistines? And Samson said unto his father, Get her for me; for she pleaseth me well. But his father and his mother knew not that it was of the Lord, that he sought an occasion against the Philistines; for at that time the Philistines had dominion over Israel.

Then went Samson down, and his father and his mother, to Timnath, and came to the vineyards of Timnath: and, behold, a young lion roared against him. And the Spirit of the Lord came mightily upon him, and he rent him as he would have rent a kid, and he had nothing in his hand: but he told not his father or his mother what he had done. And he went down and talked with the woman; and she pleased Samson well. And after a time he returned to take her, and he turned aside to see the carcass of the lion; and, behold, there was a swarm of bees and honey in the carcass of the lion. And he took thereof in his hands, and went on eating, and came to his father and mother, and he gave them, and they did eat: but he told not them that he had taken the honey out of the carcass of the lion. So his father went down unto the woman: and Samson made there a feast; for so used the young men to do. And it came to pass, when they saw him, that they brought thirty companions to be with him. And Samson said unto them, I will now put forth a riddle unto you: if ye can certainly declare it me within the seven days of the feast, and find it out, then I will give you thirty sheets, and thirty change of garments: but if ye cannot declare it me, then shall ye give me thirty sheets, and thirty change of garments. And they said unto him, Put forth thy riddle, that we may hear it. And he said unto them, Out of the eater came forth meat, and out of the strong came forth sweetness. And they could not in three days expound the riddle. And it came to pass on the seventh day, that they said unto Samson's wife, Entice thy husband, that he may declare unto us the riddle, lest we burn thee and thy father's house with fire: have ye called us to take that we have? is it not so? And Samson's wife wept before him, and said, Thou dost but hate me, and lovest me not: thou hast put forth a riddle unto the children of my people, and hast not told it me. And he said unto her, Behold, I have not told it my father nor my mother, and shall I tell it thee? And she wept before him the seven days, while their feast lasted: and it came to pass on the seventh day, that he told her, because she lay sore upon him: and she told the riddle to the children of her people. And the men of the city said unto him on the seventh day, before the sun went down, What is sweeter than honey? And what is stronger than a lion? And he said unto them, If ye had not ploughed with my heifer, ye

had not found out my riddle. And the Spirit of the Lord
came upon him, and he went down to Ashkelon, and slew
thirty men of them, and took their spoil, and gave change
of garments unto them which expounded the riddle: and his
anger was kindled, and he went up to his father's house.
But Samson's wife was given to his companion, whom he had
used as his friend.

But it came to pass within a while after, in the time of
wheat harvest, that Samson visited his wife with a kid; and
he said, I will go in to my wife into the chamber: but her
father would not suffer him to go in. And her father said, I
verily thought that thou hadst utterly hated her; therefore I
gave her to thy companion: is not her younger sister fairer
than she? take her, I pray thee, instead of her.

And Samson said concerning them, Now shall I be more
blameless than the Philistines, though I do them a displeasure. And Samson went and caught three hundred
foxes, and took fire-brands, and turned tail to tail, and put a
fire-brand in the midst between two tails. And when he had
set the brands on fire, he let them go into the standing corn
of the Philistines, and burnt up both the shocks, and also
the standing corn, with the vineyards and olives. Then the
Philistines said, Who hath done this? And they answered,
Samson, the son-in-law of the Timnite, because he had taken
his wife, and given her to his companion. And the Philistines came up and burnt her and her father with fire. And
Samson said unto them, Though ye have done this, yet will
I be avenged of you, and after that I will cease. And he
smote them hip and thigh with a great slaughter: and he
went down and dwelt in the top of the rock Etam.

Then the Philistines went up, and pitched in Judah, and
spread themselves in Lehi. And the men of Judah said,
Why are ye come up against us? And they answered, To
bind Samson are we come up, to do to him as he hath done
to us. Then three thousand men of Judah went to the top
of the rock Etam, and said to Samson, Knowest thou not
that the Philistines are rulers over us? what is this that thou
hast done unto us? And he said unto them, As they did
unto me, so have I done unto them. And they said unto
him, We are come down to bind thee, that we may deliver
thee into the hand of the Philistines. And Samson said
unto them, Swear unto me, that ye will not fall upon me
yourselves. And they spake unto him, saying, No; but we
will bind thee fast, and deliver thee into their hand: but
surely we will not kill thee. And they bound him with two

new cords, and brought him up from the rock. And when he came unto Lehi, the Philistines shouted against him: and the Spirit of the Lord came mightily upon him; and the cords that were upon his arms became as flax that was burnt with fire, and his bands loosed from off his hands. And he found a new jaw-bone of an ass, and put forth his hand and took it, and slew a thousand men therewith. And Samson said, With the jaw-bone of an ass, heaps upon heaps, with the jaw of an ass have I slain a thousand men. And it came to pass, when he had made an end of speaking, that he cast away the jaw-bone out of his hand, and called that place Ramath-lehi.

And he was sore athirst, and called on the Lord, and said, Thou hast given this great deliverance into the hand of thy servant: and now shall I die for thirst, and fall into the hand of the uncircumcised? But God clave an hollow place that was in the jaw, and there came water thereout; and when he had drunk, his spirit came again, and he revived: wherefore he called the name thereof En-hakkore, which is in Lehi unto this day. And he judged Israel in the days of the Philistines twenty years.

Then went Samson to Gaza, and saw there an harlot, and went in unto her. And it was told the Gazites, saying, Samson is come hither. And they compassed him in, and laid wait for him all night in the gate of the city, and were quiet all the night, saying, In the morning, when it is day, we shall kill him. And Samson lay till midnight, and arose at midnight, and took the doors of the gate of the city, and the two posts, and went away with them, bar and all, and put them upon his shoulders, and carried them up to the top of an hill that is before Hebron.

And it came to pass afterward, that he loved a woman in the valley of Sorek, whose name was Delilah. And the lords of the Philistines came up unto her, and said unto her, Entice him, and see wherein his great strength lieth, and by what means we may prevail against him, that we may bind him to afflict him; and we will give thee, every one of us, eleven hundred pieces of silver. And Delilah said to Samson, Tell me, I pray thee, wherein thy great strength lieth, and wherewith thou mightest be bound to afflict thee. And Samson said unto her, If they bind me with seven green withs that were never dried, then shall I be weak, and be as another man. Then the lords of the Philistines brought up to her seven green withs which had not been dried, and she bound him with them. (Now there were men lying in wait,

abiding with her in the chamber.)   And she said unto him,
The Philistines be upon thee, Samson.   And he brake the
withs, as a thread of tow is broken when it toucheth the fire:
so his strength was not known.   And Delilah said unto
Samson, Behold, thou hast mocked me, and told me lies:
now tell me, I pray thee, wherewith thou mightest be bound.
And he said unto her, If they bind me fast with new ropes
that never were occupied, then shall I be weak, and be as
another man.   Delilah therefore took new ropes, and bound
him therewith, and said unto him, The Philistines be upon
thee, Samson.   (And there were liers in wait abiding in the
chamber.)   And he brake them from off his arms like a
thread.   And Delilah said unto Samson, Hitherto thou hast
mocked me, and told me lies: tell me wherewith thou
mightest be bound.   And he said unto her, If thou weavest
the seven locks of my head with the web.   And she fastened
it with the pin, and said unto him, The Philistines be upon
thee, Samson.   And he awaked out of his sleep, and went
away with the pin of the beam, and with the web.   And she
said unto him, How canst thou say, I love thee, when thine
heart is not with me?   thou hast mocked me these three
times, and hast not told me wherein thy great strength lieth.
And it came to pass, when she pressed him daily with her
words, and urged him, so that his soul was vexed unto death,
that he told her all his heart, and said unto her, There hath
not come a razor upon mine head; for I have been a Nazarite unto God from my mother's womb: if I be shaven, then
my strength will go from me, and I shall become weak, and
be like any other man.   And when Delilah saw that he had
told her all his heart, she sent and called for the lords of the
Philistines, saying, Come up this once; for he hath showed
me all his heart.   Then the lords of the Philistines came up
unto her, and brought money in their hand.   And she made
him sleep upon her knees: and she called for a man, and she
caused him to shave off the seven locks of his head; and she
began to afflict him, and his strength went from him.   And
she said, The Philistines be upon thee, Samson.   And he
awoke out of his sleep, and said, I will go out, as at other
times before, and shake myself.   And he wist not that the
Lord was departed from him.   But the Philistines took him,
and put out his eyes, and brought him down to Gaza, and
bound him with fetters of brass; and he did grind in the
prison-house.   Howbeit the hair of his head began to grow
again after he was shaven.

Then the lords of the Philistines gathered them together

for to offer a great sacrifice unto Dagon their god, and to rejoice: for they said, Our god hath delivered Samson our enemy into our hand. And when the people saw him, they praised their god: for they said, Our god hath delivered into our hands our enemy, and the destroyer of our country, which slew many of us. And it came to pass, when their hearts were merry, that they said, Call for Samson, that he may make us sport. And they called for Samson out of the prison-house; and he made them sport: and they set him between the pillars. And Samson said unto the lad that held him by the hand, Suffer me that I may feel the pillars whereupon the house standeth, that I may lean upon them. Now the house was full of men and women; and all the lords of the Philistines were there: and there were upon the roof about three thousand men and women, that beheld while Samson made sport. And Samson called unto the Lord, and said, O Lord God, remember me, I pray thee, and strengthen me, I pray thee, only this once, O God, that I may be at once avenged of the Philistines for my two eyes. And Samson took hold of the two middle pillars upon which the house stood, and on which it was borne up, of the one with his right hand, and of the other with his left. And Samson said, Let me die with the Philistines. And he bowed himself with all his might; and the house fell upon the lords, and upon all the people that were therein: so the dead which he slew at his death were more than they which he slew in his life. Then his brethren, and all the house of his father, came down, and took him, and brought him up, and buried him between Zorah and Eshtaol, in the burying-place of Manoah his father: and he judged Israel twenty years.

APPENDIX B.

ESSAY ON METRE.

§ 1. Introduction.—The dialogue of *Samson Agonistes* is written in *blank verse*; the choruses in irregular *iambic* or *trochaic* metre, rhymed and unrhymed. The object of the present appendix is to explain these distinctions, and to point out the metrical laws which can be discerned in the play.[1]

---

[1] The books which I have found of most use in dealing with the question of Miltonic verse are R. Bridges, *Milton's Prosody* (an invaluable work), and J. B.

§ 2. **Stress.**—The possibility of verse depends mainly upon that quality of speech which is known as *stress* or *accent.* Speech is made up of a succession of *syllables*, that is, of sounds or groups of sounds, each consisting of a vowel, or of a vowel accompanied by one or more consonants, and pronounced by a single muscular effort. This succession is broken up by pauses, which range in length from the slight pause after each word to the important pause at the end of a sentence. Syllables differ amongst themselves in various manners, which depend upon variations in the complicated physical processes by which sounds are produced. We are here only concerned with two of these differences, namely, *quantity* and *stress*. The *quantity* of a syllable is measured by the time which the effort of pronouncing it takes. Syllables are classified according to quantity as *long* or *short*. Nearly all Latin and Greek metres rest upon this distinction, but in English it is of secondary importance (see §§ 8. (ii); 12. (iii)). The *stress* of a syllable is the amount of force or impulse with which it is uttered. Every syllable of course requires some of this force or impulse to be audible at all; but it is customary to speak of syllables which have more of it as *stressed*, and of those which have less as *unstressed*. Thus in the word *Dalila*, the first syllable is stressed, the last two are unstressed. *Stress* is sometimes called *accent*, and is conveniently denoted by a ('), thus, *Dá'lila*. Most words other than monosyllables have a normal stress on one or more syllables, and it is a tendency of English, as of all Teutonic languages, to throw this stress as near the beginning of the word as possible. (See, however, § 10.) Long monosyllables are also normally stressed. Short monosyllables, however, and some dissyllables have no normal stress, but are capable of receiving one, if the meaning they convey is of importance in the sentence. This deliberate imposition of a stress for the purpose of bringing out a meaning is called *emphasis.*

[*N.B.*—Some writers distinguish not merely between unstressed and stressed syllables, but between unstressed, lightly or weakly stressed, and strongly stressed syllables. As a matter of fact, the degrees of stress which a syllable is capable of receiving are more numerous than either of these classifications implies; and on this fact much of the beauty of

Mayor, *Chapters on English Metre.* Useful books on the general subject of metre are: H. Sweet, *History of English Sounds*; A. J. Ellis, *Early English Pronunciation*; J. A. Symonds, *Blank Verse*; and for those who know German, J. Schipper, *Englische Metrik*, and *Grundriss zu Englischen Metrik.* Much help may also be obtained from many of the books devoted to Shakespeare's Prosody, such as E. A. Abbott, *Shakespearian Grammar* (§§ 452-515); G. König, *Der Vers in Shakspere's Dramen*; or the Essays on the subject in the various volumes of the *Warwick Shakespeare.*

verse depends. But, for the purposes of scansion, the important thing is not the absolute amount of stress, but the relative stress of the syllables in the same foot (cf. § 3). The introduction of light stress appears to me only to confuse matters, because if you use the threefold classification, no two readers will agree in the amount of stress to be put on particular syllables: it is hard enough to get them to do so with the twofold division. Moreover, in practice, the notion of light stress has led many metrists to disregard level rhythms, such as the pyrrhic or the spondee, altogether. Yet such assuredly exist. This is not the place to discuss the subject at length, but it is right to explain my departure from usage. But let me repeat, that the limits of variation both in stress and rhythm are much beyond what any system of scansion can comprehend.]

§ 3. **Rhythm.**—Stress is a quality of speech, alike in prose and verse; and, moreover, alike in prose and verse, when stressed and unstressed syllables follow each other in such an order as to be pleasing to the ear, the result is *rhythm*. But the rhythm of verse is much more definite than that of prose. Verse consists of *feet* arranged in *lines*; that is to say, its rhythm depends upon a series of groups of syllables, in each of which groups the stress is placed according to a recognized law, while the series is broken at regularly recurring intervals by a pause. And the various kinds of rhythm, or *metres*, may be classified according to (a) the number of feet or syllables in the line, and (b) the position of the stress in the foot. The principal kinds of feet are best known by names adapted from the classical quantitative metres. They are these:—

In ascending rhythm—

Iamb.	Non-stress+stress,	as, eclípse.
Anapaest.	Non-stress+non-stress+stress,	as, in the cámp

In descending rhythm—

Trochee.	Stress+non-stress,	as, tótal.
Dactyl.	Stress+non-stress+non-stress,	as, Dálila.

In level rhythm—

Spondee.	Stress+stress,	as, úncleán, úncháste
Pyrrhic.	Non-stress+non-stress,	as, in a.
Tribrach.	Non-stress+non-stress+non-stress,	as, [insé]părăbly.

Most kinds of English verse can be *scanned*, that is, metrically analysed, as combinations of one or more of these feet in lines of different length.

§ 4. **Rhyme.**—Another quality, which may or may not be present in English verse, is *rhyme*. This is produced when the last stressed syllables of two or more neighbouring lines have the same or nearly the same sound. The ordinary form of rhyme is that in which the same vowel and final consonantal sounds are accompanied by a different initial consonantal sound; as *ring, sing.* Where there is no such

different initial consonant, the rhyme is called *identical.*
Where all the consonantal sounds differ, and only the vowel
sound is the same, as in *ring, kill,* then *assonance* and not
rhyme is produced.

§ 5. **Blank Verse.**—The metre used by Milton in the dialogue of *Samson Agonistes* is a form of the iambic decasyl-
lable or *heroic* line. This consists, normally, of five iambic
feet, with a pause after the second or third foot as well as at
the end of the line; thus:

My race' | of glor' | y run', | and race' | of shame' (397).

Such heroic lines, rhymed in couplets, form the standard
metre of eighteenth-century poetry; but Milton makes almost
exclusive use of the unrhymed heroic line, generally known
as *blank verse.* Blank verse was first used in English by the
Earl of Surrey in his translation of the Aeneid. It became
the fashion amongst the court writers of tragedy, who thought
with Sidney that to eliminate rhyme was to be classical; and
was introduced into the popular drama by Marlowe in his
Tamburlaine. Nash satirized the "drumming decasyllabon",
but the new metre proved so suitable for dramatic purposes,
that it soon relegated rhyme to a quite secondary position.
Elizabethan drama is practically a blank-verse drama. With
the Restoration, popular favour veered round to the rhymed
heroic couplet as the favourite metre for drama. Milton,
however, who in the preface to *Paradise Lost* had condemned
rhyme as "the invention of a barbarous age", made his further
protest against the new fashion in *Samson Agonistes.*

§ 6. **The Type of Blank Verse and its Varieties.**—We
have seen that a blank-verse line is normally composed of
five iambic feet, with a middle and a final pause. But to
compose an entire poem of lines rigidly adhering to this
structure would involve two difficulties. In the first place
it would produce a terrible monotony of effect; and in the
second place it would be an intolerable restraint upon expression. It would be impossible to so arrange words that they
should fall into sections of exactly equal length and exactly
similar stress, and should yet convey adequately the poet's
meaning. Therefore all writers of blank verse have allowed
themselves to deviate very considerably from the normal type,
within the limits of this general principle, that the variations
must never extend so far as to prevent that type from being
easily recognizable as that of the verse as a whole. The interpretation of this principle depends, of course, upon the ear
of the particular writer; each handles his blank verse in a

different and individual fashion. Therefore it is necessary to determine for each the limits within which his ear allows him to vary the metre of any given poem. In doing this it is well to remember that the results can only be approximate and not scientifically precise; for this reason, that just as the poet writes by ear and not by *a priori* rules, so the ear of the reader—the educated ear of the cultivated reader—is the only ultimate criterion of how any individual line is to be scanned. And though in the main such readers will agree, there will always be certain lines which can be read in two ways, one of which will sound best to one ear, one to another. It may, however, be added that in all probability we can arrive at greater precision in analysing the metre of Milton than is the case with any other great poet; and for this reason, that he would seem to have trusted less to his ear than his fellows, and to have worked by fairly definite metrical rules laid down by himself.

§ 7. **Variations in the Materials of Verse.**—But before we proceed to inquire what varieties of blank verse Milton permitted himself in *Samson Agonistes*, we have to consider another question hardly less important. In all verse the problem before the writer is to accommodate to a given type of metre words of varying stress, and a varying number of syllables have to be accommodated to metre. Where difficulties arise, two courses are open—either to modify the metre or to modify the words. For both are alike capable, within limits, of modification. The normal pronunciation of any word is that which an educated reader of careful enunciation would give to it in reading prose. But this normal pronunciation, especially as regards the number of syllables, is often modified: (*a*) dialectically, (*b*) colloquially. Thus we say '*em* for *them*, and even, I am afraid, '*cos* for *because*. And poetry has at all times claimed for itself, within certain customary bounds, a still larger license of modification. What has been said so far applies to modern as well as Elizabethan poetry. But it must be added that the bounds of this license were very much wider for an Elizabethan than they are for us. Elizabethan pronunciation, like Elizabethan grammar, was in a transition stage. Our comparative uniformity in the matter had been by no means arrived at. Even the normal pronunciation differed in many respects from ours. Thus Shakespeare regularly said *perséver*, where we say *persevére*. But in addition to this, there were many obsolete pronunciations which, though they had ceased to be normal, were still living enough not to be out of place in poetry. Some of these are inherited by Milton. Without distinguishing between licenses which are and those which are not still possible to us in verse, we will consider what amount of variation we have to allow for in reading *Samson Agonistes* from our own normal prose pronunciation. And this (*a*) as regards the number of syllables in a word; (*b*) as regards the position of stress. After which we can go on to the varieties of metre itself.

[*N.B.*—It is sometimes convenient to mark a suppressed or slurred letter by an apostrophe (*th'*), or by a dot underneath it (*ẹ*); a separately-sounded syllable by a diaeresis (¨) on the vowel, and two merged syllables by a circumflex (⌢).]

§ 8. Syllabic Variation.

(i) The unstressed *e* of the verb and noun inflections, so far as it had survived to Milton's time, was capable of being sounded or not at pleasure. In Milton, contraction is almost invariable in the case of verbal forms, except, of course, in the cases of sibilants before *-es*, *-est*, or of dentals before *-eth*, *-ed*, where the *e* is necessarily sounded. The only other exceptions I have noted are a few participles, *e.g. obeyëd* (895), *armëd* (1190), *archëd* (1634).

On the other hand, in the superlative termination *-est*, contraction is very rare. Mr. Bridges (p. 16) finds only one instance in the whole of Milton, *rugged'st* in *Paradise Regained*, ii. 164. I would add from *Samson Agonistes*, *high'st* (339).

(ii) An unstressed short vowel coming between two consonants may be elided or slurred in almost any place. This is especially the case where the vowel is followed by *l*, *n*, or *r*, which, with *m*, are known as *liquids* or *vowel-likes*. When a vowel-like follows another consonant it makes the very slightest difference in the pronunciation, whether a vowel sound is interposed or not. This may be tested by comparing the pronunciation of *able* (so written, but pronounced *abel*) and *ably*. Instances of such elision or slurring in *Samson Agonistes* are:—

(*a*) Before *l*—*popular* (16), *turbulent* (552), *miraculous* (586), *perilous* (804), *insolence* (1236). This elision, according to Mr. Bridges, explains contractions of adjectives ending in *-ble*, the *le* being treated as pronounced *ël* or *ẹl*. See the elaborate discussion on pp. 11–14 of his tract. Some instances in *Samson Agonistes* are:—

> Best pleased with humblẹ and filial submission (511).
>
> How honourablẹ, how glorious to entrap (855).
>
> This day will be remarkablẹ in my life (1388).
>
> Nothing dishonourablẹ, impure, unworthy (1424).

It is clearly, I think, the *e* that is elided by Milton, and not, as seems to be sometimes the case with Shakespeare, a vowel earlier in the word, *e.g. honourable*; but the elision might also be explained under (iv).

(*b*) Before *n* — *prisoner* (7), *burdenous* (567), *poisonous* (763), *incompassionate* (818). The past part. in *-en* might come here instead of under (i).

(*c*) Before *r* — *offering* (26), *deliverer* (40), *degenerately* (419), *slaveries* (485), *rigorous* (513), *extraordinary* (1383), *clamouring* (1621).

The following are all the instances I can discover of a similar elision before consonants other than *l*, *n*, and *r* :—

(*d*) Before *c* — *medicinal* (627), but the word may also be scanned *medicinal* (cf. note *ad loc.*).

(*e*) Before *d* — *providence* (1545).

(*f*) Before *f* — *manifest* (997).

(*g*) Before *m* — *magnanimous* (524), *enemies* (1726).

(*h*) Before *s* — *Philistines* (577).

(*i*) Before *t* — *capital* (394, 1225), *authority* (868), *indignities* (1341), *idolatrous* (1378), *idolatry* (1670), *magnanimity* (1470), *calamitous* (1480), *inevitably* (1657).

The word *spirit* requires special consideration. It occurs seven times in *Samson Agonistes*. In three of these (594, 613, 1238) it is a dissyllable; in four (666, 1269, 1435, 1675) a monosyllable. The first *i* cannot well be elided, though it comes before *r*, because it is stressed, unless we suppose that the stress is transferred to the second *i*, which would give the alternative form *sprite*. But *sprite* has its special sense, and it is better to suppose that the second *i* is elided before *t*, thus, *spirit*. Mr. Bridges (p. 10) notes that the Italians elide the cognate word *spirito* in similar fashion.

Mr. Bridges (pp. 15, 26) points out that Milton's use of such elisions in *Samson Agonistes* is an extension of his rule in *Paradise Lost*, where only elisions before *l*, *n*, and *r* are admitted, with the exceptions of *spirit*, *capital* (*Paradise Lost*, ii. 924; xi. 343), and *Capitoline* (*Paradise Lost*, ix. 508).

(iii) Some common words, pronouns, auxiliaries, prepositions, and articles suffer mutilation in various ways, and merge in colloquial combinations. Thus we have *'m* for *am*, *'ve* for *have*, *'d* for *had*, *'st* for *hast*, *t'* for *to*, *'s* for *is* and for *his*, *'t* for *it*. It is to be noticed that such colloquial contractions are far rarer in Milton than in the easier, less dignified blank verse of Shakespeare's plays; and that many of such as do occur come under the following rule (iv). Thus we have *th'* before a vowel; but very rarely *th'* before a consonant, or the forms *o' th'*, *i' th'*, though these are remarkably common in Shakespeare's later verse.   Mr. Bridges (p. 16), indeed, says that they never occur in *Paradise Lost* (except in *i' th' midst—Paradise Lost*, i. 224; xi. 432), and he mentions no relaxation of the rule in *Samson Agonistes*; but we may possibly have *Or th' sphere* (172), *To th' body's* (607), *I' th' camp* (1436), *To th' spirits* (1269), *But th' heart o' th' fool* (298).   Cf., however, § 16 (ii).

(iv) Two adjacent unstressed vowels are often merged into a single syllable; or, where a stressed and an unstressed vowel are adjacent, the latter is absorbed into the former; *y* counts as a vowel.   This takes place—

(*a*) Where the vowels are in the same word, as *laborious* (14), *curiosity* (775), *annual* (986), *fiery* (27), *being* (885), *quiet* (1724), *giant* (1181), *violating* (893), *carrying* (385).

(*b*) Where the vowels are in different words, as *I am* (1347), *I intend* (911), *me is* (70), *me under* (378), *me assassinated* (1109), *to acquit* (897), *to oppose* (862), *the ends* (893), *the utmost* (1153), *virtue as* (870), *virtue or* (756), *they effect* (681), *by itself* (769), *by importuning* (797), *pity or* (814), *any of* (1018), *justly yet* (1171), *friendly intent* (1078), *petty enterprise* (1223).

(*c*) The presence of *h*, *w*, or *wh* pronounced as *h*, does not prevent the elision, thus, *Abraham's* (29), *towards* (772), *widowhood* (958), *sorrow indeed* (1347), *thou hast* (826), *who have* (377), *to have* (627), *thou have* (783), *who had* (1622), *by his* (1305).

[*N.B.*—(1) In these elisions Milton seems to have been guided less by his ear, than by a deliberately formed rule, and as a consequence many of them appear, to some readers at least, intolerably harsh.

(2) There are, of course, a number of words in which originally distinct vowel-sounds have become *normally* merged owing to the consonantal affinities of certain vowels, *i*, for instance, passing readily into *y*. Such are *superstition* (15), *dungeon* (69), *Philistian* (216), *occasion* (224). Milton rarely uses the license, frequent in Shakespeare, especially in the earlier plays, of resolving these merged vowels back into their original two syllables.   But we have *ancient* (653), and doubtless a few others.]

(v) Certain consonants can be elided when they come between two vowels, and the vowels then coalesce into a single syllable.   These consonants are *v*, and more rarely *th*.

The only examples of this elision in *Samson Agonistes* appear to be:—

> O'er-worn and soil'd (123).
> And shall again, pretend they ne'er so wise (212).
> Some way or other yet further to afflict thee (1252).

The common forms *e'er*, *e'en*, for *ever*, *even*, do not occur in the play. *Heaven* is elided under (ii) (*b*).

[*N.B.*—I have not distinguished between *elision* and *slurring*. In the one case the sound is completely dropped; in the other it is passed over so rapidly as to be barely appreciable. But in both cases it is conventionally regarded as non-existent for metrical purposes. See the Appendix B to Mr. Bridges' Essay.]

§ 9. **Proper Names.** — These are often, especially in Shakespeare, the occasion of metrical irregularities, but they do not present any difficulty in *Samson Agonistes*. We have *Dálila*, *Mánoa*, *Hárapha*. *Philistines* is generally a trisyllable, but in 577 is contracted by the somewhat unusual elision of *i* before *s*, thus, *Philistines*. Cf. § 8. (ii) (*g*).

§ 10. **Stress Variation.**—The normal prose stress of certain words was, and to some extent still is, variable in verse.

In words of Romance origin this is often due to the conflict between the pronunciation suggested by the analogy of Latin, and that suggested by the Teutonic tendency, already spoken of (§ 2), to throw the stress as near the beginning of the word as possible. Milton is especially fond of the Latin accent. Thus we have *captíved* (33, 694), *advérse* (192), *transvérse* (209), *impúlse* (223), *contríte* (502), *instínct* (526), *contráry* (972); for the normal *cáptived*, *ádverse*, *tránsverse*, *ímpulse*, *cóntrite*, *ínstinct*, *cóntrary*, most of which Milton has elsewhere.

§ 11. **Varieties of Metre.**—So much, then, for the possible ariations in the materials which have to be disposed into metre; we come now to those of metre itself. These may take the form of (*a*) variations upon the iambic character of the foot; (*b*) variations due to the insertion of supernumerary extra-metrical syllables; (*c*) variations due to mutilation of a foot; (*d*) variations in the number of feet in the line; (*e*) variations in the number and position of the pauses.

§ 12. **Non-Iambic Feet.**
(i) *Spondee and Pyrrhic*. Lines containing the complete number of five iambic feet are comparatively rare. When several of these occur together, they produce an effect of regular rise and fall which is stiff and unnatural.

In order, therefore, to produce a more natural rhythm, *level stress* is introduced into one or more feet. That is to say, the unstressed and stressed syllables of the iamb are replaced by two stressed syllables (*spondee*), or two unstressed syllables (*pyrrhic*): thus :—

Vain' mon'- | ument | of strength'; | till length' | of years' (570).

Here the first foot is a spondee, the second a pyrrhic.

The principle which limits all variations in blank verse is that the general character of the rhythm must not be destroyed. Too many pyrrhics or spondees would make the verse altogether too light or too heavy. As a rule, therefore, we do not find more than six or less than three stressed syllables in a line, nor more than three unstressed syllables together. In *Samson Agonistes* the solemn character of the subject-matter accounts for some excess of stressed syllables; *e.g.*—

O' dark', | dark', dark', | amid' | the blaze' | of noon' (80).

I' know' | no' spells', | use' no' | forbid'- | den arts' (1139).

(ii) *Trochee.* Frequently the normal order of non-stress and stress is inverted, that is to say, a *trochee* replaces the iamb. This substitution is made most easily after a pause, and therefore it is by far the most common in the first foot, and next to that in the third and fourth, after the mid-line pause. It is rare in the second and fifth feet.

1st foot. Bon'dage | with ease' | than stren' | uous li'- | berty (271).

2nd foot. For his | peo'ple | of old'; | what hin'- | ders now'? (1533).

3rd foot. No', I' | am fix'd' | not' to | part hence' | without' (him)(1481).

4th foot. Suffi'- | ces that | to me' | strength' is | my bane' (63).

I do not readily find an instance of a trochee in the fifth foot.

Two trochees may occur in a line, not, as a rule, in succession. More than two would tend to obscure the iambic character of the rhythm.

Ease' to | the bo'- | dy some', | none' to | the mind' (18).

No'thing | is here' | for tears', | no'thing | to wail (1721).

Milton makes a special use of a double trochee in the first and second feet. This is said to be due to the influence of Italian models.

That' in- | vin'ci- | ble Sam- | son, far | renown'd (341).

§ 13. **Feminine Rhythm.** — Sometimes an extra-metrical unstressed syllable is added after the stress, before a pause.

The result is known as *feminine* rhythm. It is most common at the end of the line, thus:—

> In what part lodged, how easily bereft (me) (48).
>
> And lamentation to the sons of Caph(tor) (1713).

Feminine rhythm in the middle of the line is rare in Milton. Mr. Bridges (p. 7) does not admit it in *Paradise Lost*, and he does not name it as one of the points in which *Samson Agonistes* differs from *Paradise Lost*. I think, however, that we have a clear instance in:

> Bet'ter | at home' | lie bed'-(rid), not' on- | ly i'(dle) (579).

And I think that a similar scansion is the natural one in:

> She pur'- | posed to | betray' (me); | and', which | was worse' (399).
>
> Depos'- | ited | within' (thee); | which' to | have kept' (429).
>
> Out', out', | hyae'(na)! | These' are | thy wont'- | ed arts' (748).
>
> Or by | eva'(sions) | thy crime' | unco' | ver'st more' (842).

as well as in the following choric line:

> In sla'- | vish hab'(it), | ill'-fit'- | ted weeds' (122).

It is, however, possible to explain all these lines except line 579 by somewhat forced elisions, as *me͡ and, which to͡ have, Hya͡ena*, or *thy͡ wonted* (cf. Mr. Bridges, p. 30), *by͡ evasions habit*.

§ 14. **Varieties of Pause.**—The typical heroic line has a well-marked pause at the end, and a less well-marked one in the middle, after the second or sometimes the third foot. These are, of course, sense pauses, as well as metrical pauses. Milton modifies this original type in two principal ways—

(i) He varies the mid-line pause at will, omitting it altogether, or making it as slight as possible, or doubling it, or putting it after the first or fourth foot, or in the middle of a foot.

[*N.B.*—Some writers call the mid-line pause a *caesura*. This is, of course, hopelessly incorrect. The classical *caesura* was a slight pause in the middle and not at the end of a foot.]

(ii) He reduces the importance of the end-line pause, which can never altogether disappear, by putting the two separated lines in close syntactical connection. Such a connection is called an *enjambment*, and the first of the two lines is said to be *run on*, as opposed to *end-stopped*. Consider, for instance, lines 1708–12 :—

Come, come ; no time for lamentation now,
Nor much more cause: Samson hath quit himself
Like Samson, and heroically hath finished
A life heroic, on his enemies
Fully revenged ; hath left them years of mourning.

Here the first line and the last are end-stopped, the second,
third, and fourth run on.   Of course it is largely a matter of
degree; the enjambment is more or less marked, according
as it is affected by various conditions, the weight of the syntactical parts separated, the closeness of the syntactical
connection, the presence of feminine rhythm, and the like.
The effect of this redistribution of pauses is to destroy the
independence of the single line by making it a member of an
harmoniously-arranged group, a period or verse-paragraph.
Through this a less monotonous rhythm becomes possible.

It is curious that we do not find in *Samson Agonistes*, as
we do in Shakespeare's early plays, that special use of the
end-stopped line, in which a rapid dialogue is carried on by
each speaker confining what he has to say to the limits of a
line: curious, because this device corresponds so closely to
the *stichomuthia* of Milton's model, the Greek tragedy.   The
nearest approach to it is in such short passages as lines
1345–7.

Milton rarely divides a line between two speakers.   He
does so to mark the nervous excitement of Manoa and the
Messenger in 1563, 1584, 1586.

§ 15.   **Regularity of the Blank Verse.**—Milton avoids monotony in the blank verse of *Samson Agonistes* by the free use
of spondees, pyrrhics, and trochees, and by the greatest
variety in the distribution of his pauses.   He does not admit
the greater irregularities which we are accustomed to in the
plays of Shakespeare—monosyllabic feet, Alexandrines, lines
of one, two, three, or four feet.   Nor does he admit trisyllabic
feet, anapaests, dactyls, and tribrachs, such as cannot be resolved, by slurring or elision, into the equivalents of iambs,
trochees, and pyrrhics.   Nor does he admit rhyme.   The
rhyme in 1519–20 appears to be an exception.   On the ap-
parent irregularity of 496–7, see note *ad loc.*   This is partly
because the tone of Milton's drama is far more stately and
less colloquial than is usual with Shakespeare; partly because
it was essential to preserve a contrast between the blank verse
and the choruses, in which it was his design to produce a
lyric character by the use of just such devices.

§ 16.   **The Choric Metre.**—The choruses are made up of
two kinds of line.

(i) *Iambic* lines, differing from those of the blank verse in four points:

> (a) The lines are of varying lengths, from one to six feet, the latter being known as Alexandrines.
> (b) Rhyme is occasionally introduced.
> (c) Trochees are proportionately more numerous.
> (d) Anapaests are occasionally introduced: cf. below in (ii).

(ii) *Trochaic* lines, in which the trochees are not merely introduced to vary the iambs, but in which they so preponderate as to give their character to the whole rhythm of the line. These lines occur here and there amongst the iambic ones; they are not very numerous, but I find the following:—

> Let' us | not' break | in' up- | on' him (116).
> That' her- | o'ic, | that' re- | nowned' (125).
> O' that | tor'ment | should' not | be con- | fined' (606).
> But' must | se'cret | pas'sage | find' (610).
> As on | en'trails, | joints', and | limbs' (614).
> And ce | les'tial | vig'our | arm'd' (1280).
> Great' a- | mong the | hea'then | round' (1430).
> While' their | hearts' were | jo'cund | and sub- | lime' (1669).
> Like' that | self'-be- | got'ten | bird' (1699).
> In the Ar- | a'bian | woods' em- | boss'd' (1700).
> That no | sec'ond | knows' nor | third' (1701).
> All' is | best', though | we' oft | doubt' (1745).
> Oft' he | seems' to | hide' his | face' (1749).

It will be observed that the unstressed syllable of the last foot is more often than not omitted.

Mr. Bridges (pp. 35, 36) would add these, which I prefer to scan as iambic lines varied by the introduction of anapaests:

> Or' the | sphere' of | for'tune | rais'es (172).
> To' the | bo'dy's | wounds' and | sores' (607).
> As' a | lin'ger- | ing' dis- | ease' (618).
> Like' a | state'ly | ship' (714).
> In' the | camp' of | Dan' (1436).

I should scan:

> Or̄ the sphere' | of For'- | tune rais'(es).
> To̅ the bo'- | dy's wounds' | and sores'.
> As̄ a lin'- | gering | disease'.
> Likē a state'- | ly ship'.
> In̄ the camp' | of Dan'.

I also find anapaests in :

    Irreco'- | vera- | bly dark', | to'tal | eclipse' (81).

    For his peo'- | ple of old'; | what' hin'- | ders now' (1533).

    To the spi'rits | of just' | men long' | oppress'd' (1269).

There are two in :

        But the heart' | of the fool' (298).

Some, however, of these anapaests may be resolved into iambs if we admit the license of *th'* for *the* before a consonant (cf. § 8 (iii.)).

It appears to have been Milton's object, without losing in the choruses the solemnity and stateliness which characterize his blank verse, to introduce into them just such rhythms and cadences as would give them, compared with that, a slightly lyrical effect.

APPENDIX C.

MILTON'S ENGLISH IN SAMSON AGONISTES.

[*N.B.—The student who wishes to go further into the subject may refer to Dr. Edwin Abbott's Shakespearian Grammar and to the chapters on Milton's English in Professor Masson's various editions of Milton.*]

§ 1. **Introduction.**—The object of this Appendix is to bring together certain points in which Milton's English, and particularly his syntax, differs from what we should now consider good prose English. It is necessary to remember that the rules or customs of modern English were only settled by the practice of the great eighteenth-century writers ; and that therefore we must not expect to find them holding good either in the prose or poetry of an earlier date. And with Milton in particular we have to bear in mind the existence of two sets of tendencies, in some respects contradictory, both of which were strong in him, but which unite in making his English different from our own.

(*a*) Milton was throughout his life a careful student of the Latin authors. As Latin Secretary under the Commonwealth, he habitually composed both letters and pamphlets in the Latin tongue (cf. Introduction, p. 10). Naturally this had its effect upon his English style. His thought, diction, and syntax are all Latinized. We find him translating Latin idioms, alien to English. We find him using participles (§§ 5 (b), 6) and relatives (§ 5 (d)) in the Latin fashion. And, more generally, we find him modelling his sentences upon the long Latin sentence or period with its elaborate apparatus of principal and subordinate clauses.

(b) But secondly, Milton inherited the English of the Elizabethans with what appears at first sight its disregard of rule and syntax altogether. Elizabethan English, as we find it in Shakespeare, is English in a transition stage. The old English, the highly-inflected English of Chaucer, had been broken down; the new uninflected English of the eighteenth century had not yet been set up. In the meantime, a crowd of new ideas and feelings had come in with the Renascence, and were clamouring for expression. The result was that Elizabethan writers wrote very much as they pleased, unfettered by rule, and aiming at brevity and clearness, far more than at grammatical accuracy.

We are mainly concerned here with syntax, but it is worth while, first of all, to point out briefly how these two tendencies, the Latin and the Elizabethan, affected Milton in the use of individual words.

§ 2. Latinism in Individual Words.—This chiefly shows itself in the use of words derived from the Latin, not in their English or 'derivative' sense, but in their original Latin or 'radical' sense.

(a) Thus *diffidence* (454), *diffused* (118), *exercise* (1287), *expedition* (1283), *fallacious* (320), *miracle* (364), *notice* (1536), *ornate* (712), *prime* (70), *secular* (1707), *secure* (55), &c. Cf. Glossary, s.vv.

(b) Similarly we find words which are usually adjectives treated by Milton as what they originally were, participles. Instances are: *separate* (31) = 'separated' (Lat. *separatus*); *ornate* (712) = 'adorned' (Lat. *ornatus*); *frustrate* (589) = 'frustrated' (Lat. *frustratus*).

§ 3. Elizabethanism in Individual Words.

(a) Dr. Abbott (*Shakespeare Grammar*, p. 5) points out that "almost any part of speech can be used as any other part of speech". We have—

i. Nouns used as verbs or participles, and expressing any possible relation between the idea of the noun so used and that of some other: thus—

charioting (27) = 'removing in a chariot'; *proverb'd* (203) = 'made the subject of proverbs'; *lorded over* (267) = 'behaved as lords over'; *gloried* (334) = 'glorious'; *principled with goodness* (760) = 'having good principles'; *garrison'd* (1497) = 'placed in garrison'; *perched roosts* (1693) = 'roosts upon which birds perch'; *bolted* (1696) = 'sent a bolt'. Similarly *a living death* (100) = 'a death united with life'; *blandish'd parlies* (403) = 'parlies carried on in a blandishing tone'; *warbling charms* (934) = 'charms uttered in a warbling tone'.

ii. Nouns used as adjectives : thus—

a bosom-snake (763); *politician lords* (1195).

iii. Adjectives used as adverbs : thus—

causeless (701), *fix'd* (726), *whole* (809), *plain* (1256), *fat* (1671), *speedy* (1681), for *causelessly, fixedly, wholly, plainly, to fatness, speedily.*

(*b*) Certain superlatives are formed by the use of inflections which a modern writer would form by the aid of *most*: thus—

constantest (848), *famousest* (982), *oftest* (1030), *solemnest* (1147).

(*c*) Certain conjunctions and prepositions are used in ways now discarded. We have—

to wail (66) = 'for the wailing'; *that* (759) = 'so that'; *because they shall not* (1402) = 'in order that they may not'.

(*d*) The normal sense of certain suffixes seems to be forgotten; thus we have *deceivable* (350), which should mean 'able to be deceived' in the sense of 'deceiving': cf. *Richard II.,* ii. 3. 84, "Whose duty is deceivable and false". In 'painful diseases and deform'd' (699), *deform'd* practically = 'deforming'.

§ 4. **Peculiarities of Syntax.**—It is almost impossible to classify these as Latinisms and Elizabethanisms. Both the tendencies which affected Milton led to a greater brevity of speech than is now normal; led, in fact, to what grammarians call ellipses.

§ 5. **Ellipses.**

(*a*) The subject of a verb is sometimes omitted :

"Then by main force [he] pull'd up, and on his shoulders bore
The gates of Azza, post and massy bar" (146, 147).

"Thou wilt say,
Why then [I] reveal'd [it]?" (799, 800).

Abbott (*Sh. Gr.,* §§ 399–402) explains this, partly by a lingering sense of O.E. inflections, partly by Latin influence, partly by the rapidity of Elizabethan pronunciation, which frequently changed *he* into *a'* and prepared the way for dropping *he* altogether.

Masson quotes—

> "His trust was with the Eternal to be deemed
> Equal in strength, and rather than be less
> [He] Cared not to be at all " (*P. L.*, ii. 46–48).

Cf. also *Winter's Tale*, iv. 4. 168:

> "They call him Doricles: and [he] boasts himself
> To have a worthy feeding".

(*b*) The object of a transitive verb is omitted:

> "Why then [I] reveal'd [it]?" (800).

> "Chanting their idol, and preferring [him]
> Before our living Dread" (1672, 1673).

> "Which to have merited, without excuse,
> I cannot but acknowledge [myself]" (734, 735).

> "Which argues [him] over-just, and self-displeased" (514).

> "Knowing [myself], as needs I must, by thee betray'd" (840).

The first three instances explain themselves; the fourth is parallel to the use of the Latin *arguere*='prove', 'betray'; *e.g.* Horace, *Epod.*, xi. 9:

> "In quis amantem languor et silentium
> Arguit ".
> ('Amongst whom my languor and my silence prove [me] in love'.)

The fifth seems due to the influence, not of a Latin, but a Greek construction, the use of a participle with verbs of perception, as αἰσθανόμεθα γελοῖοι ὄντες ('We perceive [ourselves to be] ridiculous').
The stock Miltonic instance is:

> "And knew not [herself to be] eating death ' (*P. L.*, ix. 792).

(*c*) An auxiliary verb is omitted, *e.g.*:

> "[To be] Blind among enemies! O worse than chains" (68).
> "pretend they [to be] ne'er so wise" (212).
>   "though my pardon
> [Be] No way assured" (738, 739).
> "By his habit I discern him now
> [To be] A public officer" (1305, 1306).

The explanation may be sometimes the Elizabethan desire for brevity, sometimes the influence of Latin constructions. Thus the third example would correspond to the Latin *quamvis* or *licet* with an ablative absolute.

(*d*) The antecedent of a relative is omitted, *e.g.*:

> "Like [him] whom the Gentiles feign to bear up Heaven" (150).

> "Unless there be [those] who think not God at all" (295).

> "Rise therefore with all speed, and come along,
> [There] Where I shall see thee hearten'd and fresh clad" (1316–7).

This is, of course, a Latinism: cf. "Qui haec videbant fle-
bant" ('[Those] Who saw this, wept').

Sometimes the antecedent is a personal pronoun understood from a possessive pronoun, *e.g.*:

> "As vile hath been my folly, who have profaned
> The mystery of God" (377, 378).

This is really one of the constructions 'according to sense
described under § 8. 'My folly' = 'the folly of me': cf.:

> "which might in part my grief have eased,
> Inferior to the vilest now become" (72, 73).

(*e*) By the omission of *of*, a phrase compounded of a noun
and an adjective does duty as an adjective:

> "frock of mail
> [Of] Adamantean proof" (133, 134).

This is a pecularly Miltonic idiom. It is akin to the use of
nouns as adjectives already spoken of (cf. § 3. (*a*) ii). Prof.
Masson quotes:

> "his ponderous shield,
> [Of] Ethereal temper, massy, large, and round" (*P. L.*, i. 284, 285).

> "feather'd mail,
> [Of] Sky-tinctured grain" (*P. L.*, v. 284, 285).

> "Under his forming hands a creature grew,
> Man-like, but [of] different sex" (*P. L.*, viii. 470, 471).

(*f*) There are various ellipses, not falling under any of
these heads:

> "[The] Promise was that I
> Should Israel from Philistian yoke deliver" (38, 39).

> "nor was I their subject,
> Nor under their protection, but my own;
> Thou [under] mine, not theirs" (886–888).

> "I . . . presumed
> [To raise] Single rebellion, and did hostile acts" (1209, 1210).

> "To himself and [to his] father's house eternal fame" (1717).

> "From whence [resulted] captivity and loss of eyes" (1744).

An attempt to translate these sentences into Latin will in
most cases show the source of the idiom.

§ 6. **Participial Constructions.**—Milton's Latinism is most clearly shown in the free use he makes of participial constructions.

(*a*) He uses what is known as the nominative or accusative 'absolute', *i.e.* a phrase compounded of a noun and a participle, taking the place of an adverbial clause:

> "if I must die
> Betray'd, captived, and both my eyes put out" (32, 33)
> = 'if I must die, after both my eyes have been put out'.

> "Dagon hath presumed,
> Me overthrown, to enter lists with God" (462, 463)
> = 'now that I am overthrown'.

> "that maxim . . . prevailed
> Virtue, as I thought, truth, duty, so enjoining" (870)
> = 'Since virtue, &c., so enjoined'.

> "What if, his eyesight (for to Israel's God
> Nothing is hard) by miracle restored,
> He now be dealing dole among his foes" (1527–1529)
> = 'after his eyesight has been restored'.

This construction corresponds exactly to the Latin use of the 'ablative absolute'; cf. 'Caesar, acceptis litteris, proficisci constituit' ('Caesar, after he received the letter, determined to set out').

(*b*) Somewhat similarly, a participle used as an adjective takes the place of an adverbial clause, *e.g.*:

> "restless thoughts . . . no sooner found alone
> But rush upon me thronging" (19–21)
> = 'as soon as I am found alone'. The 'but' is superfluous, and to be explained under § 8.

> "which in his jealousy
> Shall never, unrepented, find forgiveness" (1375, 1376)
> = 'if it is unrepented'.

> "he may dispense with me, or thee,
> Present in temples at idolatrous rites" (1377, 1378)
> = 'although we are present'.

This also is due to Latin idiom; cf. 'Epistulae offendunt, non loco redditae' ('Letters annoy, if they are not delivered in season').

In Milton, as in Latin, an adverbial clause is sometimes introduced by a relative. Cf.:

> "overpower'd
> By thy request, who could deny thee nothing" (880, 881)
> = 'since I could deny thee nothing',

with "Caesar, qui haec omnia explorata haberet, redire statuit" ('Caesar, since he had full knowledge of all this, decided to return').

(*c*) A participle takes the place of a verbal noun:

"prevented by thy eyes put out" (1103)

= 'by the putting out of thy eyes'.

"He must allege some cause, and offer'd fight
Will not dare mention" (1253, 1254)

= 'the offering of fight'.

"Rode up in flames after his message told
Of thy conception" (1433, 1434)

= 'after telling his message'.

Cf. also "sight bereaved" (1294) = 'the loss of sight'; "eye-sight lost" (1489); "My countrymen, whom here I knew remaining" (1549).

The stock Latin instance is 'Post urbem conditam' = 'after the founding of the city'.

A similar construction is found in:

"O mirror of our fickle state,
Since man on earth, unparalleled" (164, 165)

= 'Since the creation of man', or, as Milton elsewhere has it, "since created man" (*P. L.*, i. 573).

§ 7. **Inversions.**—Milton is occasionally obscure, because of the freedom with which he inverts the natural order of the parts of his sentences; a freedom which all poets permit themselves, but he, influenced by the Latin practice, most of all. Thus:

"Who this high gift of strength committed to me,
In what part lodged, how easily bereft me,
Under the seal of silence could not keep" (47–49).

Here the natural order is, 'Who could not keep under the seal of silence in what part this high gift of strength committed to me [was] lodged, [and] how easily [it was] bereft me'.

"for with joint pace I hear
The tread of many feet steering this way" (110, 111)

= 'For I hear the tread of many feet steering this way with joint pace'.

"The rest was magnanimity to remit" (1470)

= '[it] was magnanimity to remit the rest'.

"no preface needs" (1554)

= '[there] needs no preface'.

§ 8. **Changes of Construction.**—Milton adopted the long Latin sentence, but he did not adopt with it the strict Latin syntax. Many of his sentences, in fact, will not bear analysis into principal, co-ordinate, and subordinate clauses at all. Like the Elizabethans, he was content to be clear—and his meaning is generally obvious enough—without aiming at precise grammatical accuracy. Many of his constructions are therefore what is called κατὰ σύνεσιν, according to sense; that is, they depend on the meaning rather than on the formal expression of what has gone before. His sentences are not, like Latin sentences, thought out beforehand on a logical plan, which is strictly adhered to; they are piled up, clause upon clause, in the loosest grammatical connection, as new thoughts, additions to or qualifications of his first thoughts, occur to him. Or, if we like, we may put the matter, with Abbott (*Sh. Gr.*, § 415) and Masson, thus: that Milton, like Shakespeare, often changes the construction of a sentence midway, as a result of some transition of thought which has occurred while he is in the course of it. Two or three instances will help to explain this.

> "Many are the sayings of the wise,
> In ancient and in modern books enroll'd,
> Extolling patience as the truest fortitude,
> And to the bearing well of all calamities" (652–655).

Here Milton writes the last line as if he had said in the line before, 'Exhorting to patience'; and this is *the sense*, though not *the letter* of what he did say.

> "had not spells,
> And black enchantments, some magician's art,
> Arm'd thee or charm'd thee strong, which thou from Heaven
> Feign'dst at thy birth was given thee in thy hair" (1132–1135).

Here we may say that Milton writes the second clause as if the first had been 'had not spells given thee strength', or, which is the same thing, that the relative depends for its antecedent upon the idea of 'strength' understood from 'arm'd thee or charm'd thee strong'.

> "Although their drudge, to be their fool or jester,
> And in my midst of sorrow and heart-grief
> To show them feats, and play before their god—
> The worst of all indignities" (1338–1341).

Here the last clause is an afterthought, put as a comment in apposition to the whole of what precedes.

> "Others more moderate seeming, but their aim
> Private reward" (1464, 1465).

Here the second clause, according to the original design of the sentence, should have been 'but aiming at private reward'. To this what Milton does say is an exact equivalent in sense, but not in form.

>   "God had not permitted
> His strength again to grow up with his hair
> Garrison'd round about him like a camp
> Of faithful soldiery, were not his purpose
> To use him further yet in some great service—
> Not to sit idle with so great a gift
> Useless, and thence ridiculous, about him" (1495–1501).

According to the strict grammatical construction, it is God, and not Samson, who is 'not to sit idle'. Milton has, in fact, shifted his thought in the last clause to a new grammatical subject; and the whole is equivalent to, 'Samson is to do some further service, and not to sit idle'.

The student is advised, whenever he comes upon a sentence, the construction of which is not at once obvious to him, first of all to try analysing it in the ordinary way; and if this fails, to study it until he has satisfied himself of the nature of the transition in Milton's thought which took place while it was being written.

GLOSSARY

---

abstruse (1064), enigmatic, from Lat. *abstrusus*, concealed.

accident (612), symptom; a technical term of medicine.

acquist (1755), acquisition. The form is derived not from Lat. *acquisitio*, but Med. Lat. *acquistum*, a form of the part. *acquisitum*.

adamantean (134), hard as adamant. *Adamant*, through Lat. from Gk. ἀδάμας, untamable, irresistible, was used both for the diamond, from its hardness, and the loadstone, from its attractive force.

address (731), preparation. So, too, **address'd** (729), prepared, lit. made straight, from O. F. *adressier*, L. L. *addrictiare*, Lat. *directum*, straight.

advise (328), consider, deliberate.

aggravate (1000), add to, make worse; lit. 'pile up a load', from Lat. *ad*, to, *gravare*, to load, *gravis*, heavy. So, too, **aggravation** (769).

amain (637, 1304), lit. with might; *a* being a degenerate form of the prep. *on*, and *main*=A.S. *maegen*, strength. The word is used as an intensifying adverb; thus 'comes on amain' = 'comes on with speed', 'thrived amain' = 'thrived exceedingly'.

amaze (1645), amazement; cf. *Hymn on Nativity*:
"The stars with deep amaze
  Stand fix'd in steadfast gaze".

Milton uses either form indifferently.

amber (720), ambergris or gray amber, a substance secreted by the whale, of which perfumes were made; quite distinct from what we now know as *amber*, a yellow fossil gum.

antic (1325), jester, clown; probably so called from the 'antic' (*antiquus*=quaint, fantastic) dress or gestures of such entertainers.

appellant (1220), challenger. An appeal was the technical mediaeval term for a challenge to judicial combat.

appoint (373), determine, dispose. Some editors take it in the sense of **tax** (210), *q.v.*

apprehensive (624), sensitive.

argue (514, 1193), prove; a common sense of Lat. *arguere*.

assay (392, 1625), essay; the two forms are respectively from O. F. *assai*, *essai*, Lat. *exagium*, weighing, trial. The form *assay* is now retained only in the special sense of a testing of coin or metals.

ay me (330), alas! woe is me! the O. F. *aymi*, Ital. *ahimé*, Span. *ay de mí*, Gk. οἴ μοι. The *me* is here, like the Gk. μοι, an 'ethic' dative.

baffled (1237), disgraced; connected with F. *bafouer*, mock, Low Sc. *bauchle*, vilify; a chivalric term, used of a punishment in-

140   SAMSON AGONISTES

flicted on recreant knights, and described in Spenser's *Faerie Queene*, vi. 7. 27:

" He by the heels him hung upon
    a tree,
And baffull'd so that all which
    passed by
The picture of his punishment
    might see ".

The modern sense is rather 'thwart'.

baits (1538), rests, lit. of a traveller, 'gives his horses food', from M. E. *beiten*, Icel. *beita*, make to *bíta*, bite or feed.

bane (63, 351), harm, from A. S. *bana*.

bank (1610), apparently used here in the sense of the Fr. *banc*, a bench.

bed-rid (579), confined to bed, from M. E. *bedrede*, a corruption of A. S. *bedrída*, a bed-rider.

blab (495), tell tales, prate, from M. E. *blaberen*, Dan. *blabbre*, to babble, an onomatopoeic word.

blandish'd (403), flattered, soothed, from O. F. *blandir*, Lat. *blandiri*, caress.

blank (471), dismay, lit. blanch, make white, from F. *blanc*, white.

blazed (528), announced, proclaimed, as by the blowing of trumpets, from M. E. *blasen*, A.S. *blaesan*, to blow.

bolt (1696), fall in a bolt; used as a verb, of thunder.

boot (560), avail; in the phrase 'it boots'; **boot**, profit, help, is the A. S. *bót*, compensation.

bravery, i. (717), ornament, finery; the adjective *brave* is common in the same sense; ii. (1243), boasting, ostentatious courage.

brigandine (1120), coat of mail, lit. armour for a brigand, from F. *brigand*, Ital. *brigante*, robber, Ital. *briga*, strife.

brunt (583), onset, attack; a M. E. word from Icel. *bruna*, to rush on like fire, *brenna*, to burn.

cataphract (1619), a horse-soldier, through Lat. from Gk. κατάφρακτος, covered up (with mail).

chafe (1246), passion, temper.

charioting (27), bearing away, as in a chariot.

circumstance (1557), details.

compare (556), comparison.

connive (466), wink, in the sense of the Lat. *connivere*, with an allusion to *Acts*, xvii. 30: "the times of this ignorance God winked at".

craze (571), crush, break down; connected with F. *écraser*.

crude (700), premature. "Crude old age" is taken, though with a changed sense, from the " *iam senior, sed cruda deo viridisque senectus*" of Virgil, *Aeneid*, vi. 304.

deceivable (350, 942), deceitful. Shakespeare uses the word in the same sense and no other; cf. *Milton's English*, § 3 (*d*).

deform'd (699), apparently for 'deforming'; cf. *P. R.*, iii. 86: "Brutish vices and deformed". And *Milton's English*, § 3 (*d*).

deject (213), depress, in the common sense of the part. *dejected*.

descant (1228), consider from all sides. 'Descant' as a musical term meant to play or sing variations upon a given melody.

diffidence (454), want of faith, distrust, in the sense of the Lat. *diffidentia*.

diffused (118), spread out, in the sense of the Lat. *diffusus*.

disordinate (701), disorderly, dissolute.

dispose (1746), disposal.

distract (1556), distracted.

dole (1529), pain, from the Lat. *dolore*.

doughty (1181), in the compound **tongue-doughty**, bold, valiant, from A. S. *dyhtig*, bold, is from *dugan*, to avail, be worth.

draff (574), refuse, especially the food of swine.

embattled (129), in array of battle.

emboss'd (1700), hidden in a wood; properly embosked, from F. *embosquer*, Ital. *imboscare*, to shut up in a *bosco*, bush, wood.

enforce (1223), difficulty.

engine (1396), instrument, means.

estate (742), state, condition.

event (737), issue, result, in the sense of Lat. *evenire*, to turn out, happen.

exercise (1287), discipline, practice, in the sense of the Lat. *exercere*.

expedition (1283), swiftness, in the sense of Lat. *expedite*, lit. without impediment.

expiate (736), atone.

exulcerate (625), inflame, raise ulcers or sores.

fallacious (320), deceitful, in the sense of the Lat. *fallax*.

fix'd (1481), determined.

fond (1682), foolish.

forgery (131), forging, in the lit. sense of metal.

forgo (940), go against; *for* is used, as in *forsake*, like the Ger. *ver*, which adds a bad sense to the verb it is compounded with. In *forego*, go before, the prefix= Ger. *vor*.

fraught (1075), freight, cargo.

garrison'd (1497), placed in garrison.

gauntlet (1121), glove of mail.

genial (594), natural; a man's genius is properly his familiar spirit, and so his nature or disposition.

gin (933), snare, a shortened form of engine.

gloss (948), interpret falsely, from Gk. γλῶσσα, in the sense of an explanation of a difficult word written in the margin.

greaves (1121), the part of a suit of armour protecting the lower part of the leg.

grounded (865), established, built on firm ground.

gymnic (1324), gymnastic, from Gk. γυμνικός.

gyves (1093), fetter; connected with *gefyn*.

habergeon (1120), breastplate, more strictly neck-guard; from O. F. *hauberjon*, a dim. of *hauberc* = O. H. Ger. *halsberc*, *i.e.* a neck-protection; *hals*=neck, *bergen*= protect.

hamper (1397), impede, literally maim; from M. E. *hamperen*, a variant of *hamelen*, A.S. *hamelian*.

harbinger (721), forerunner; M. E. *herbergeour*, O. F. *herberg-er*, one who provided lodgings for a man of rank.

hearten'd (1317), encouraged, put into heart; we use *dishearten'd* in the opposite sense.

her (71, 613), **his** (612), used as the genitive of the neuter pronoun, though indeed 'light', 'mind', 'torment' may be regarded as personified. The A. S. forms of the gen. were *his*, *hire*, *his*, from the noms. *he*, *heo*, *hit*. By the 16th century *hit* became *it*, and the gen. *his* for neut. as well as masc. seemed anomalous. For some time *it* and *her* were tried, or the use of the gen. was avoided.

Its first appears late in the 16th century and was not at first popular. It is rare in the *A.V.* and in the *First Folio* of Shakespeare. Milton only uses it three times; in *Nat. Ode*, 106; *P.L.*, i. 254; iv. 813. Elsewhere he uses *his* or *her*. Cf. Abbott, *Sh. G.*, § 228; Craik, *English of Shakespeare*, p. 91; Masson, *Library Milton*, I, lviii.

high (1458, 1599), in the phrase 'the high street', where it seems to mean first 'principal' as opposed to 'bye', and then public, open. *Highway* has a similar meaning, and there is a 'High Street' in most towns.

hold (802), restraint.

holocaust (1702), an offering of a whole beast; the Gk. ὁλόκαυστον, used in the Sept. to translate a Hebrew word = 'a whole burnt-offering', from ὅλος, whole, καίειν, to burn.

idolists (453), idolaters; a form apparently due to analogy with 'atheists'.

immedicable (620), incurable, the sense of the Lat. *immedicabilis.*

importune (775), troublesome in begging, a more correct form of 'importunate'; from Lat. *importunus*, troublesome.

impulsion (422), impulse.

incident (656, 774), liable to occur, from Lat. *incidens*, part. of *incidere*, to come upon.

incorporate (161), unite, become one (lit. one *corpus* or 'body') with.

infest (423), attack; lit. *infestare.*

inform (335), give information to, direct.

inhabitation (1512), in the phrase 'the whole inhabitation' =

'all the inhabitants', abstract for concrete.

inherit (1012), originally 're-ceive as heir', then generally (1) 'get possession of'. Cf. *Romeo and Juliet*, i. 2. 28, 'inherit at my house'; (2) 'be in possession of'.

inseparably (154), unalterably, for ever. Cf. *P.L.*, iv. 472:

"him thou shalt enjoy
Inseparably thine",

interlunar (89), belonging to the *interlunium*. Cf. note *ad loc.*

intermission (1629), interval, rest; lit. *intermissio*, from *intermittere*, leave off, pause.

intimate (223), within the soul, from Lat. *intimus*, innermost.

invocate (1146), invoke, im-plore, call upon a deity for aid, a common sense of Lat. *invocare.*

irruption (1567), breaking in, the Lat. *irruptio*, from *in*, and *rumpere*, to break.

join'd (1342), fastened, a com-mon sense of Lat. *jungere.*

laver (1727), basin, from Lat. *lavare*, to wash. It is the term used in *A.V.* of *Exodus*, xxx. 18, etc., for the basin used for ritual purposes in the court of the Temple.

legal (313), according to the law, in the special sense of the Law of Moses.

lists (463), 'The space enclosed by barriers in which tournaments or single combats took place.' From Low Lat. *liciae*, 'barriers'; perhaps connected with *licium*, 'thread'; thus *lists* would be originally 'a space roped in'. So too **listed** (1087), set out with lists.

lord (267), behave as a lord. Cf. *Milton's English*, § 3 (a) i.

magnified (440), glorified; the

Lat. *magnificatus*, lit. made great, from *magnus*, great, *facere*, make.

manacle (1309), fetter; lit. a fetter for the hand, from F. *manicle*, Lat. *manicula*, dim. of *manica*, hand-cuff, from *manus*, hand.

massy (1633), a shortened form of *massive*.

mean (207), moderate, second-rate.

mimic (1325), actor. Cf. *Midsummer-Night's Dream*, iii. 2. 19, "And forth my mimic comes".

mind (1603), have in mind, intend, wish.

miracle (364), object of wonder; the first sense of Lat. *miraculum*, from *mirari*, to wonder.

motion (222), have in mind. Cf. *P. L.*, ix. 229, "Well hast thou motioned". Apparently suggested by the Lat. *motus animi*, but *motio animi* is not so used. Cf. also *P. L.*, vi. 192, "no sight, nor motion of swift thought".

mummer (1325), masquerader; from O.F. *mommeur*; O. Du., *mommen*, to go a-mumming. Skeat says that "the word is imitative, from the sound *mum* or *mom*, used by nurses to frighten or amuse children, at the same time pretending to cover their faces".

mystery (378), divine secret; from Gk. μυστήριον, a name given to certain secret rites in the worship of Demeter and other divinities.

nerve (639), muscle, the 'sinew' of modern English, whereas the Elizabethan *sinew* often corresponds rather to our 'nerve'.

notice (1536), knowledge, in the sense of the Lat. *notitia*.

obnoxious (106), exposed to, liable to, in the usual sense of the Lat. *obnoxius*.

obsequy (1732), funeral rite: more usual is the plural obsequies, and the Lat. is always *obsequiae*.

obstriction (312), bond, obligation, from Lat. *obstringere*, to tie up.

obvious (95), in the way, exposed. In the sense of Lat. *obvius*; from *ob*, in front of, *via*, a way.

occasion (1596), business.

on (1118), over.

ornate (712), adorned, in the sense of Lat. *ornatus*.

over-watch'd (405), worn out by watching or sleeplessness.

paranymph (1020), friend of the bridegroom—the modern 'best man'. The Gk. παράνυμφος, prob. a variant for παρανύμφιος, from παρα, beside, νυμφίος, a bridegroom.

parle (785), parley, interview, conference; from F. *parler*, speak, a military term.

part (1481), depart.

perched (1693), in the phrase "perchèd roosts", roosts where birds perch.

pernicious (1400), destructive. The Lat. *perniciosus*.

perverse (737), contrary to expectation; from Lat. *perversus*, awry, askew; *per*, around, *vertere*, turn.

pitch (169), height; a metaphor from falconry, in which the word denoted the height to which a hawk soared before it swooped.

politician (1195), intriguing. *Politic* is similarly used in *P. R.*, iii. 398-400:

"think not thou to find me
   .   .   .   need
Thy politic maxims",

said by Christ to Satan.

pomp (1312), sumptuous festivity. Perhaps with a reminiscence of the sense of Lat. *pompa*, Gk. πομπή, a solemn procession.

post (1538), hastily: lit. with relays of horses. Originally *a post* is the station where relays were kept for the use of letter-carriers (whence our modern sense) and others.

power (251), an armed force.

presage (1387), foreboding. Lat. *praesagium*, from *prae*, before, *sagire*, to feel intensely.

prescript (308), decree. Lat. *praescriptum*, lit. something written beforehand, from *prae*, before, *scribere*, to write.

prime (70, 85, 234), first, in sense of Lat. *primus*.

prone (1459), low down, humble, lit. on one's face, in the sense of Lat. *pronus*.

proof (134), strength, lit. armour that has been proved or tested. Cf. *Richard III.*, v. 3. 218, "Ten thousand soldiers armed in proof"; *Richard II.*, i. 3. 73, "Add proof unto mine armour with thy prayers"; *Hamlet*, ii. 2. 512, "Mars' armour, forged for proof eterne".

propense (455), disposed, in sense of Lat. *propensus*, lit. hanging forward, from *pro*, forward, and *pendere*, to hang.

propose (1200), ask, lit. put forward; from Lat. *pro*, forward, *ponere*, to put.

proverb'd (203), spoken of in proverbs. Cf. *Milton's English*, § 3 (*a*) i.

quit (324, 509), free of debt; from M. E. *quiten*, L. Lat. *quietare*, *quietus*, in special sense of 'clear of debt'; lit. at rest, quiet.

ramp (139), spring; from F. *ramper*, to spring, lit. to climb. Cf. *Psalm* xxii. 13, "a ramping and a roaring lion".

ravel (305), become confused. The metaphor, however, is not from a tangled, but from a frayed thread. Woven or twisted things are said to 'ravel' when the strands part; cf. *Richard II.*, iv. 1. 288:

"Must I ravel out
My weaved up follies?"

redundant (568), superfluous, in sense of Lat. *redundans*, lit. overflowing.

refer (1015), consider, trace out, in a sense of the Lat. *referre*.

regorged (1671), gorged, stuffed; the Lat. *re* having, as in *redundant*, an intensive force. In "fat regorged", fat is an adjective used as an adverb. Cf. *Milton's English*, § 3 (*a*) iii.

relation (1595), a report, account; in a late sense of Lat. *relatio*, and the common one of English *relate*.

remark (1309), point out, distinguish, in the ordinary sense of *remarkable*.

reprobate (1685), erroneous. Used in A. V. of *Romans*, i. 28, for Gk. ἀδόκιμος, spurious.

respect (868), consideration.

rift (1621), split; a verb derived from a noun. Cf. *Milton's English*, § 3 (*a*) i.

robustious (569), vigorous. In using the term of hair, Milton may have in mind *Hamlet*, iii. 2. 10, "O, it offends me to the soul to hear a robustious periwig-pated fellow tear a passion to tatters".

rout (443), a disorderly crowd, lit. a mass of broken troops. The Lat. *rupta*, part. of *rumpere*, to break.

rueful (1553), piteous.

ruin, i. (1514), destruction, ii. (1515), lit. a fall of buildings, a common sense of Lat. *ruina*, from *ruere*, to rush, tumble.

score (433), debt; lit. a notch scored or cut in a tally, and so a tavern reckoning.

secular (1707), long-lived, age-long, from Lat. *secularis*, adj. of *seculum*, an age.

secure (55), self-confident in sense of Lat. *securus*, which generally implies a mistaken sense of security.

sensibly (913), sensitively.

sentence (1369), maxim, in a sense of Lat. *sententia*.

separate (31), set apart, with the participial force of Lat. *separatus*, from *separare*.

signal (338), remarkable, noticeable.

sinew (1142), probably in modern sense of muscle, though in Elizabethan English it more often equals nerve, while *nerve* equals our muscle.

single (1092), single out, pick out for single combat. Cf. *3 Hen. VI.*, ii. 4. 1: "Now, Clifford, I have singled thee alone".

sort (1608), rank. Cf. *Much Ado*, i. 1. 7: "Few of any sort and none of name".

specious (230), beautiful, in sense of Lat. *speciosus*, which has often already the modern sense of deceitfully beautiful, plausible.

state (424), enter into the details of, discuss. Johnson defines 'state' as to "represent in all the circumstances of modification".

stupendious (1627), a form of *stupendous*.

suage (184), a shortened form of *assuage*.

subscribe (1535), agree; lit. write one's name at the bottom of; from Lat. *sub*, beneath, *scribere*, to write.

subserve (57), serve; 'sub', as in the last word, having the meaning 'beneath'.

supposing (1443), expecting.

surcease (404), cease; but the word is not etymologically connected with *cease*, being from O. F. *surseoir*, to pause, Lat. *supersedere*, refrain from, lit. to sit upon, from *super*, upon, *sedere*, to sit.

surfeit (1562), excess, more than enough. The O. F. *surfait*, *sorfait*, part. of *sorfaire*, to exagerate, from Lat. *super*, above, *facere*, to make.

taste (1091), test, try.

tax (210), criticise, lit. meddle with, handle, from F. *taxer*, Lat. *taxare*, a form of *tactare*, the frequentative of *tangere*, to touch.

teem'd (1703), born, from M. E. *temen*, to give birth, *tem*, offspring.

temper, i. (670), rule, lit. mingle, in sense of Lat. *temperare*; ii. (133), of steel, to harden by dipping in water, also from Lat. *temperare*, to mix, in sense of mixing wine with water.

tend (1302), approach, come, in sense of Lat. *tendere*.

thrall (370, 1622), serf, from Dan. *træl*, lit. runner.

toil (933), snare; from F. *toile*, Lat. *tela*, a web.

train (533, 932), snare, trick. Cf. *Macbeth*, iv. 3. 118:

"Devilish Macbeth
By many of these trains hath
sought to win me
Into his power".

The verb is similarly used. Cf. *Comedy of Errors*, iii. 2. 45:

"Train me with thy note, to
drown me".

The der. is from F. *traîner*, to draw.

transverse (209), out of the straight path, in sense of Lat. *transversus*.

treat (482), do business, come to terms, in sense of F. *traiter*, and Eng. *treaty*.

triumph (1312), a public show of rejoicing, from Lat. *triumphus*, the entry of a victorious general.

unconscionable (1245), excessive, lit. unconceivable, beyond the grasp of conscience, in the sense of judgment or thought.

uncouth (333), strange, lit. unknown, from A.S. *un*, not, and *cuð*, part. of *cunnan*, to know.

unjointed (177), disconnected.

uxorious (945), usually fond of one's wife, here in a depreciatory sense, 'subject to one's wife'.

van (1234), vanguard.

vant-brace (1121), the part of a suit of armour protecting the arm. From F. *avant-bras*, the 'a' being dropped.

venereal (533), seductive, lit. connected with Venus the goddess of love.

villatic (1695), belonging to a country house, Lat. *villaticus*.

vitiated (389), corrupted, the Lat. *vitiatus*.

voluble (1307), rapid, used, like the Lat. *volubilis*, of speech. We now talk rather of a voluble speaker.

weeds (122), clothes, from A.S. *wæd*.

withal (58), nevertheless, at the same time.

wont (1487), are accustomed. 3rd pers. plu. pres. of *won*, A.S. *wunian*. The verb was still conjugated by the Elizabethans; we now only use the participle and say 'are wont', just as we say 'are used to', where the Elizabethans said 'use to'.

BLACKIE'S ENGLISH TEXTS

Edited by W H. D. ROUSE, Litt.D.

General Literature

ADDISON—Essays from " The Spectator ".
The Story of Sir Roger de Coverley.

Adventures on the Seas by English Sailors in the Great Days of Old.

ÆSOP—Fables from Æsop.

BACON—Essays. 37 of the Essays.

BOCCACCIO—Tales from the Decameron.

BORROW—Gipsy Stories.
The Stories of Antonio and Benedict Mol.

BOSWELL—Life of Johnson.

BUNYAN—Pilgrim's Progress. Part I.

CARLYLE—The Hero as Divinity; Man of Letters.
The Hero as Poet: as King.

CERVANTES — Don Quixote (abridged).

COBBETT—Rural Rides.

COWLEY—Essays.

DEFOE — Captain Singleton's Ear'y Adventures.
Journal of the Plague Year.
Robinson Crusoe.

DELONEY—Thomas of Reading and John Winchcombe.
The Gentle Craft.

DE QUINCEY—The English Mail Coach, &c.

DICKENS—A Christmas Carol.
The Chimes.
The Cricket on the Hearth.

DICKENS & COLLINS — The Wreck of the " Golden Mary ".

MARIA EDGEWORTH—Castle Rackrent.

Election Scenes in Fiction.

GEORGE ELIOT—The Mill on the Floss (abridged).

ERASMUS—The Praise of Folly.

MRS. GASKELL—Cranford.

GOSSE—The Romance of Natural History.

LADY CHARLOTTE GUEST—Stories from The Mabinogion.

NATHANIEL HAWTHORNE—Tanglewood Tales.

HERBERT OF CHERBURY—Life of Lord Herbert of Cherbury. Autobiography.

HUGO—The Toilers of the Sea.

WASHINGTON IRVING—England's Rural Life and Christmas Customs.
Rip Van Winkle, &c.

KINGSLEY—The Heroes.
The Water-Babies.

LAMB—Adventures of Ulysses.
Tales from Shakspeare.

LUCIAN—Trips to Wonderland.

MALORY—Coming of Arthur.
The Knights of the Round Table.

HERMAN MELVILLE — Moby Dick: or, The Whale.

MILTON—Areopagitica, &c.

MORE—Utopia.

MOTTE - FOUQUÉ — Sintram and his Companions.

PEPYS -- Passages from the Diary of Samuel Pepys.

POE—The Gold Bug, &c.

RUSKIN—Byzantine Churches of Venice.
Crown of Wild Olive.
Sesame and Lilies.

ANNA SEWELL—Black Beauty. Part I.

SWIFT—Gulliver's Travels.

THEOPHRASTUS—Characters.

WALPOLE — Letters on the American War of Independence. Letters on France and the French Revolution.

BLACKIE'S ENGLISH TEXTS—*Contd.*

Travel

ANSON — The Taking of the Galleon. From *Lord Anson's Voyage Round the World* (1743).

BOSWELL—The Journal of a Tour to the Hebrides with Samuel Johnson, LL.D.

SIR FRANCIS DRAKE—The World Encompassed (1628).

LORD DUFFERIN — Letters from High Latitudes.

HAKLUYT — The French in Canada.

SIR RICHARD HAWKINS—Voyage into the South Sea.

EVARISTE RÉGIS HUC — A Sojourn at Lhassa.

WASHINGTON IRVING — Companions of Columbus.

CAPTAIN JAMES—The Voyage of Captain James (1633).

POLO — The Travels of Marco Polo.

SAMUEL PURCHAS — Early Voyages to Japan (1625).

RALEIGH—The Discovery of Guiana.

SMITH, B. WEBSTER—Pioneers of Exploring.

History

BEDE—History of the Church of England. Down to A.D. 709.

ROBERT BLAKENEY—The Retreat to Corunna.

Britain and Germany in Roman Times.

PHILIPPE DE COMMINES — Warwick the Kingmaker.

FROISSART—Border Warfare under Edward III and Richard II.
Crecy and Poitiers.

HOLINSHED—England in the Sixteenth Century.

RICHARD KNOLLES — Wars with the Turks.

MACAULAY—Macaulay's History. Chapter I. Before 1660. Chapter II. Under Charles II.
Essay on Clive.
Essay on Hastings.
Essay on Hampden.
Second Essay on Pitt, Earl of Chatham.
Essay on Sir William Temple.

AMMIANUS MARCELLINUS—Julian the Apostate.

MONTLUC—The Adventures of Montluc.

MOTLEY—William the Silent. Alva (1567-8).

NAPIER—Battles of the Peninsular War. 2 vols.
1. Coruña, Talavera, Badajos.
2. Salamanca, Siege of Burgos, Vittoria, Siege of San Sebastian.

LORD NELSON—The Battle of the Nile. Dispatches and Letters.

ORME—The Black Hole of Calcutta and the Battle of Plassey.

PLUTARCH—Life of Pompey. Themistocles and Pericles. Aristeides and Marcus Cato. Alexander. Julius Cæsar. Brutus and Coriolanus.

PRESCOTT—Montezuma. The Capture of Mexico.

JOHN SMITH—Early History of Virginia (1627).

THUCYDIDES—The Siege of Syracuse.

WALPOLE—Letters on the American War of Independence. Letters on France and the French Revolution.

DUKE OF WELLINGTON—Waterloo. Dispatches of Wellington, &c.